Seeking the Future in the Past

Seeking the Future in the Past

But there are women I'd been close to in my earlier years, and I've often been curious about what has happened in their lives, and I'm going to try to reconnect with some. As you know, I dated and married your mother several years after graduating college. Still, before I met Pietrina, I was involved in three serious relationships—or as serious as can be when young—one in the last year of high school and slightly beyond, one late in my sophomore to senior year of college, and the third when I started my first job. I looked for them on Facebook, but they could be under their married names."

"Dad, you're only in your fifties, too young to retire," Bethany said.

Alex joked, "I've had an AARP card for years."

"Did Mom share your interest in resurrecting the past and contacting old friends, especially women, when you were married?" Merry's tone was mildly mocking.

"No, not at all. Your mother was a caring person but not what I'd call sentimental. She thought the past was something you left behind. She was never interested in contacting good friends who'd moved away. Pietrina grew up in a beautiful home near a lake, and as an only child, she'd inherited the house. I encouraged her to keep it as a vacation place, but she simply refused, 'Too many memories.' I think that's also why she wanted me to take our house while she purchased the condo after we separated. Besides, I never thought about contacting these women until recently, and not while I was married."

Merideth said, lowering her eyebrows and squinting, "Are you looking to restart an old relationship? If you're trying to find someone, you should look forward, not backward.

Alex answered, "Merry, I'm not looking for a relationship, just satisfying curiosity and providing a reason for travel with a destination and purpose. I grew up in a nearby town, bought a house, and started a business. We went away for vacation or visited relatives when you were kids but did little traveling beyond that; my business prevented long trips. Now I want to see other parts of the country and know about people's lives in those places, rather than going to tourist locations by myself, or following an itinerary and trailing a bored guide."

"You could be disappointed. Many years have passed; they won't look like or be like the women you knew. What if they have no interest in meeting up with an old boyfriend or—" Merideth said before her sister interjected.

"Or even remember you," Bethany added. "I agree with Merry. You need to look ahead and find someone to add to your life, not chase after a woman from your youth."

Seeking the Future in the Past

James Hanley

A Wings ePress, Inc.
Romance Novel

Wings ePress, Inc.

Edited by: Jeanne Smith
Copy Edited by: Bev Haynes
Executive Editor: Jeanne Smith
Cover Artist: Trisha FitzGerald-Jung
Images: Pixabay

Wings ePress Books
www.wingsepress.com

Copyright © 2023 by: James P. Hanley
ISBN 978-1-59088-634-2

Published In the United States Of America

Wings ePress, Inc.
3000 N. Rock Road
Newton, KS 67114

Dedication

To Lyn, the inspiration for all my writing

One

"I'm putting on a tie my wife of twenty-four years bought me, and five years later, I'm wearing the tie again for my ex-wife's wake—and it's the same woman." His daughter reminded him he was talking to himself—a habit that became disturbingly more frequent.

"Dad," a young woman said as she pushed the partially closed bedroom door, "are you ready to go?"

Alex O'Rourke stepped from the closet and momentarily stopped to look at his daughter, Bethany, entering the room. She was a striking young woman—a blend of genetically formed features, a decade of braces, and a nagging dance teacher who emphasized posture and bearing. Bethany's trim athletic body also came from riding horses and playing on her high school soccer team.

Despite the dermatologist's warning, a fanatical devotion to tanning darkened her skin, and her luminous eyes were undimmed by the contacts she wore. In her senior year at Bridgewater College, Bethany was twenty-one and lived about fifty miles away. Her older sister, Merideth, was twenty-four, married, and living about eighty miles from his house.

Bethany said, "I heard what you said aloud, and it's strange for me to be going to Mom's funeral with my father to console her now-husband, Brian." Her eyes were on the edge of tears. "Merry said she'll meet us at the funeral home. I don't know why we call her that; my sister is the most serious person I know, and her husband is as somber as the funeral director."

"You're the one who reduced her name—she wanted to be called Merideth, no diminutive. Just remember, she's your sister."

"I love her, but," her lips formed into a grin, "I wouldn't invite her to a fun party. It would be like bringing a candle snuffer to a birthday party."

Alex grinned. "I'm glad I'm paying for your English degree so you can learn similes. I'm looking forward to seeing her. We don't get together often; even our calls are infrequent. She preferred visiting your mother and her new husband."

Bethany walked toward her father and pulled up the sleeves of his suit jacket so the cufflinks were visible. Putting her hand on his shaved cheek, she said, "Going to be a tough afternoon."

He placed his hands on her shoulders, turned her to face the stairs, and guided her out of the bedroom.

As Alex pulled up, Merideth was waiting in front of the massive doors to the funeral home, pacing on the concrete steps. Stepping down, she first hugged her sister and then her father, leaning into him, her lower back extended out. "You're late," she admonished.

Merideth's frown did little to diminish her beauty—her eyes were more circular than her sister's, but contained the same luminosity. Her facial features were well-formed, like her sibling's but without the same symmetry as Bethany's. When her lips were neutral, there was a slight downturn at the corners, unlike Bethany's, which seemed never to lose the edge of a smile.

Merideth didn't share her sibling's devotion to browning, keeping her skin a pale color altered only by tan makeup. The two could swap clothing and had been nearly the same height growing up. The front of her form-fitting dress had a slight bulge, and as they walked into the building, Bethany slowed her sister and whispered, "Are you—?"

"No, I'm not," Merideth snapped. "I'm tired of being asked. I have a sedentary job."

When they approached the room where the casket was placed, Alex and his daughters instinctively lifted their upper lips and broadened their nostrils as the smell of flowers wafted over them. Merideth first spotted the widower, Brian, and charged toward him, causing him to back up a step from the push of the embrace. She cried pent-up tears and repeated, "I'm so sorry." Bethany moved toward him, and since Merideth hadn't released her hold, the younger sister gripped his arm and said, "Sorry."

Alex shifted back and forth, looked at the closed coffin, and stared at the framed picture on top of the wood. He always knew the source of their children's beauty, and his ex-wife's attractiveness was apparent in the photograph.

After attorneys had sorted out details of the divorce, he and Pietrina had settled into an amicable relationship and had divided the house and holdings without discord. Still, their communication had been mainly by phone in the last few years, and he'd never observed her physical decline, although Merry and Bethany had both said "Mom doesn't look right."

Turning his head, he saw Brian approach, his hand extended in greeting. Alex liked his ex-wife's husband and felt he was well-suited for Pietrina. As her health had declined in the year before her death, Alex frequently called to find out how she was doing, and he'd often spoken to Brian.

Despite the man's academic appearance: goatee, slight stoop, horn-rimmed glasses, and a pleasant face, Brian owned several gas stations and garages. Alex suppressed a grin when he recalled Bethany's habit of secretly looking at the man's fingernails as if searching for black residue. The two now-former spouses of the deceased briefly conversed until interrupted by the minister's arrival to lead the eulogy. When Alex walked toward the second row of folding chairs, he saw his youngest kneeling in front of the coffin, her shoulders shaking.

~ * ~

Walking out, Alex talked to his daughters on the steps and into the parking lot. Bethany asked, "You're going to the burial tomorrow, right?"

Merideth interjected before he could respond, "It's okay if you're busy."

Noticing his younger daughter reddening, he answered, "No, I'm not going. Brian will need your support." As Alex walked away, he glanced backward and saw Bethany gesticulating at her sister. Alex lowered his head and proceeded to his car. Waving to his daughters as he pulled out of the lot, he saw both form a quick smile.

Alex slept poorly that night and into the following week. Unshaven and lingering in his pajamas, he called work one day to tell his secretary he wouldn't be coming in. She said, "It's your company; you can do what you want."

After showering and dressing, he went to Pietrina's gravesite. The mound over the plot still rose above the ground; rain began to fall, darkening the dirt and forming a small puddle over the soft earth dug to hold her tombstone to be placed later that week. He was talking but with no audible words, mouthing each sentence. When the rain came down hard, soaking his flattened hair and his face, the moisture dripped off his forehead, blending with the grief overflowing from his eyes.

~ * ~

Alex walked across the second-floor hallway of his house and stopped in front of his daughters' rooms. Bethany's room was unchanged, still filled with childhood dolls, a poster of boy singers and young athletes, soccer uniforms thrown on the chair, scuffed floors from practicing dance, and her high school graduation tassel nailed to the wall. In contrast, Merideth's bedroom was sparse: a covered bed, a corner chair and a bare nightstand were the only remnants of her time there before marrying. He remembered his older daughter completing a ritualistic purging of childhood at each stage in her life, as if removal were essential to maturing. She had taken some of the pieces after she married.

Alex's house was on a mound that sloped down to the edge of his property, flattening at a stretch of trees, blocking the homes on the other side until winter, when the splintered view of other houses reappeared. Early falling leaves gathered around roots, and sections of bare earth formed into a light brown cover, pressed in recent heavy rain; a slow-moving stream cut through the woods behind his property. Summer was fading in southern Pennsylvania, and the entry into autumn was showing. In a few weeks, the season's colors would take over from the ubiquitous green, and tourists would drive down the side roads with cameras protruding from passenger-side windows of cars with license plates from the Virginias and Maryland.

Two

His daughters were back to their lives: Bethany in college, Merideth to her job and husband, so he was surprised when the younger called and said she wanted to come home for a long weekend. "Merry can make it, too. I'll leave here Saturday morning, and my sister will get there as soon as possible. Her husband, Taylor, is at some nerdy convention, and we'll spend the night and go back Sunday afternoon. It'll be like old times." She paused before adding, "Almost."

"Good, honey, I want to talk to both of you."

"What about, Dad? Are you feeling okay?" Her voice quivered slightly.

"I'm fine. I didn't mean to frighten you, and rather than share with you alone, I'd like to talk to you both."

"Oh," she stretched the word. "You don't want to make Merry feel she's your second favorite—which you and I know is true."

Alex could tell she was teasing by the slightest change in his daughter's pitch. However, he regretted mentioning the need for a shared conversation, knowing Bethany would immediately call her sister, and the two would speculate: "What does Dad want to talk to us about?"

~ * ~

The sisters arrived within an hour of each other, and Alex asked what was new in their lives. Bethany mentioned she was working on a paper she could use for a graduate school thesis and hinted at a boyfriend. Merideth complained about her job and said she and Taylor were looking at houses.

"Okay, small talk is done," the younger said. "Why did you want us both to be here?"

"Why don't we go to lunch and talk there."

As if rehearsed, their shoulders slumped in unison. Before they could get out the door, the phone rang.

"I'll get it," Merideth chirped. After the greeting, her face broke into a huge smile.

"Taylor," Bethany explained to her father.

Merideth, her voice lowered as she conversed, stopped, put her hand over the receiver, and said, "Why don't you two go to the restaurant. I'll drive over as soon as I'm finished."

Bethany whispered, "She doesn't want us to hear their mushy talk: 'I miss you, I love you, can't wait—"

"I get it," Alex interrupted. "Let's go, Bethany."

The waitress, a weary, middle-aged woman, approached father and daughter and handed them plastic-coated menus. The waitress saw Bethany put her hand on the back of Alex's head and say, "You need a haircut." His daughter noticed the waitress frown, and, after her father ordered soft drinks to start and the woman left, Bethany leaned over and whispered, "Our waitress thinks you're robbing the cradle." Alex said, "Dad, you are still a handsome guy, with some gray hairs, wrinkles, a bit of a paunch, and you don't look your age."

Alex laughed at the mixed assessment.

Merideth arrived fifteen minutes later. "That was Taylor."

"You told us," Bethany said.

The waitress returned, her eyebrows lifting as she looked at the three. Father and daughters ordered, and the siblings pounced. "What is it you wanted to talk to us about?"

"I need you just to listen—no interruptions." He was looking at Bethany when he spoke.

"He's got a girlfriend and probably wants to marry her. Timing's not great, right after Mom's buried," Merideth said.

Bethany kicked her sister under the table.

"No, that's not it, Merry. I'm selling my business and retiring."

Merideth leaned back in her chair, and the front legs lifted. Her mouth opened, but she didn't speak.

Alex continued. "I've been in the insurance business since I graduated college, and frankly, I'm tired. Don't ask me questions about what I'm going to do next—I'll explain."

Despite the conditions he'd set, the two sisters poured out questions, speaking over each other.

"Let me answer what I think you're wondering. First, I'm not selling the house and moving away. You're also wondering: what will I do with myself? I deal with many people, and your mother and I cultivated many good friends, especially through work—my job and your mom's.

"But there are women I'd been close to in my earlier years, and I've often been curious about what has happened in their lives, and I'm going to try to reconnect with some. As you know, I dated and married your mother several years after graduating from college. Still, before I met Pietrina, I was involved in three serious relationships—or as serious as can be when young—one in the last year of high school and slightly beyond, one late in my sophomore to senior year of college, and the third when I started my first job. I looked for them on Facebook, but they could be under their married names."

"Dad, you're only in your fifties, too young to retire," Bethany said.

Alex joked, "I've had an AARP card for years."

"Did Mom share your interest in resurrecting the past and contacting old friends, especially women, when you were married?" Merry's tone was mildly mocking.

"No, not at all. Your mother was a caring person, but not what I'd call sentimental. She thought the past was something you left behind. She was never interested in contacting good friends who'd moved away. Pietrina grew up in a beautiful home near a lake, and as an only child, she'd inherited the house. I encouraged her to keep it as a vacation place, but she simply refused, 'Too many memories.' I think that's also why she wanted me to take our house while she purchased the condo after we separated. Besides, I never thought about contacting these women until recently, and not while I was married."

Merideth said, lowering her eyebrows and squinting, "Are you looking to restart an old relationship? If you're trying to find someone, you should look forward, not backward.

Alex answered, "Merry, I'm not looking for a relationship, just satisfying curiosity and providing a reason for travel with a destination and purpose. I grew up in a nearby town, bought a house, and started a business. We went away for vacation or visited relatives when you were kids but did little traveling beyond that; my business prevented long trips. Now I want to see other parts of the country and know about people's lives in those places, rather than going to tourist locations by myself, or following an itinerary and trailing a bored guide."

"You could be disappointed. Many years have passed; they won't look like or be like the women you knew. What if

they have no interest in meeting up with an old boyfriend or—
" Merideth said before her sister interjected.

"Or even remember you," Bethany added. "I agree with Merry. You need to look ahead and find someone to add to your life, not chase after a woman from your youth."

"I've had some dates since the divorce, but none that lasted," Alex said. "This is not a quest to renew a prior relationship. I've got plenty of time, and it seems an interesting project."

In near unison, the sisters showed disagreement. "This is just a *project*?" Merry asked.

"Considering the timing, does this have anything to do with Mom's death?" Bethany inquired.

"No, no. You're too young to understand. I've had time to think, and the prior events and people of your life enter your thoughts and may arouse your curiosity. Sometimes, music or a place triggers nostalgia, and you speculate on the individuals you once knew and cared about. I realize I have to look forward, but a respite in personal history could be the needed pause before taking on future challenges. I have no regrets about marrying your mother and the life that followed, especially when our love brought you two into my life."

"You're right about one thing, Dad, we don't understand, but it's your decision," Bethany said.

Alex said, " I've arranged for services to the house, like lawn care, and set up automatic payments for bills. My mail is being forwarded to your place after two weeks, Merry, one of you needs to check the house periodically. Either of you can go through the house quickly and leave, or stay over if you'd like. I don't plan to make one very long trip to visit all three at once, and will be back and forth." He reached into his pocket and handed a key to Merideth. "Bethany, you have a key."

"It doesn't seem we can talk you out of it; your mind appears set," Merideth said. "Do you know where any of these women live?"

"That's the other favor," Alex said. "Help me track them down, although I do have a lead on the first of my list. You two are better at using social media sources and researching information about people. Bethany, you were into family history and found lots of information about past relatives. Merideth can help if needed."

"I can't stay long to start scanning the internet, Dad," Merideth said. "Taylor called to tell me the convention was boring, and he was leaving to be home late today. I think he just misses me."

Bethany made a gagging sound.

"I don't have to leave until tomorrow, so I can be here for another day. I am better with computer sources than my sister."

The waitress asked if they wanted anything else, and since there was no interest, she said she would be back with the check. Before she left, the woman paused and looked at the sisters. As she started toward the cashier, Bethany whispered to Merry, "Repeat what I say before she gets too far." Merideth looked at her sibling and shrugged her shoulders. "Thank you, Dad," Bethany said loudly, and Merideth said the same.

"Okay, what was that about?" Merry asked.

The younger sister whispered, "Before you came, I put my fingers in Dad's hair to point out he needed a haircut just as the waitress handed us a menu. She gave Dad and me an odd look, probably thinking our father was robbing the cradle. I don't know what she thought when you arrived."

As soon as she explained, the waitress returned, leaning over a bit more than needed to hand him the bill.

Alex looked at the bill as he withdrew his wallet and showed his daughter the paper. Both daughters muffled their laughter. The woman's name and a phone number were on the back. They teased their father endlessly on the ride back to the house. "You don't have to travel to meet women, Dad; just eat out more," Bethany joked.

~ * ~

After a few hours at the house, Merideth hugged her father and sister before walking to her car. The breeze picked up, and the tree branches swayed in a rhythmic movement. Father and the younger daughter went inside, and Bethany told Alex she had a paper to do, was tired, and would help him start looking in the morning.

Alex remembered his daughter was a late sleeper and was surprised when she came down the stairs at seven. She wore pajamas she kept at the house, claiming they were too juvenile for a college student. The bottoms ended mid-ankle, and the top left exposed about two inches of her stomach. She stumbled toward the coffee with the urgency of someone hurrying toward a desert oasis.

"What's the game plan, Dad?" she asked cheerfully.

"I was hoping you could track down my high school girlfriend, Carolyn Lipinski."

"First, you have to tell me about her."

"Okay." Alex leaned back in his chair and lifted the coffee cup to his lips. "She was beautiful, short, intelligent, and animated. I think she felt sorry for me. I was lanky, nerdy, and socially inept. We started dating in our senior year of high school; she was my prom date. We had enrolled in colleges, and while we talked about giving up our choices and going to the same university, both sets of parents forbade the changes. She went to Iowa State with ambitions to be a writer; in the first year of college, she found she was a good writer, but not great. I went to New York University intending to go into investment banking, but that never happened."

"You didn't try to keep in touch?"

"We did and, of course, saw each other during holidays and the summer. But we knew the relationship was over at Christmas of our sophomore year."

"And you never saw her again?"

"I did. We lived in the same town but far enough away from each other that we never met during school breaks for the remaining years in college, even by accident. I got an invitation to attend the fifteenth anniversary of my high school graduation and was going to decline, but your mother talked me into going."

"That was Mom. I bet she stayed home because of her daughters."

Alex smiled and continued. "I saw Carolyn at the reunion. We talked for a long time, and the conversation was enjoyable. She was still attractive and charming and also engaged. I was so flustered when I first saw her at the event that I handed her my business card after we shook hands. There were times while I was in college and after, I regretted we had never stayed in touch." After a pause, he quickly added, "Of course, not after I married your mother."

Bethany laughed at his awkwardness. Her eyes brightened. "Was Carolyn your first sexual experience?"

"How about we talk about *your* sex life?" he answered.

Bethany bit gently on her lower lip, saying, "Did she say what her job was and where she was living?"

"I remember she said she was selling real estate, but I don't know where. When we were dating, I often went to her house, and I recall the address, but apparently, her parents sold the home or passed away. Is that enough to go on?"

"This won't be easy, especially since you had no luck on Facebook and, I assume, on other social media sites," Bethany said, "but I'll do what I can. I have to leave this afternoon; if I'm unsuccessful today, I'll keep at it while I'm at school."

"Great!" Alex exclaimed. "I'm getting dressed and going into the office for a few hours. I normally don't work on Sunday, but there's much to do before handing it over to the agency. I can wait until you leave."

"No, don't. I'll be on the computer for the rest of the morning and afterward, head back."

Alex was on the phone in the afternoon when a call came through. His secretary picked up the second line, and Alex heard her say, "I'll check and see how long he might be."

Standing in his doorway, she whispered, "Your daughter's on the phone."

Alex shortened the call and picked up the other line. "Getting ready to leave, honey?"

"Dad, Dad, I found—" The words ran so close together Alex said, "Slow down."

He heard her breathe in. "I found your old girlfriend, Carolyn."

"How did you do it, and so quickly?"

"I had a hunch she, like most young women, wanted to be married in her hometown church. That's still a custom, even now. You'd written her parents' address on a pad in your desk drawer, so I googled nearby churches and called their offices, figuring they'd be open on Sunday. After introducing myself, I explained why I was trying to track down Carolyn Lipinski. A woman in a Lutheran church was pleased to help and thought it was nice, even romantic. To my surprise, she began whispering and told me she'd heard your old girlfriend had divorced. Glad she was a gossip! Carolyn's last name is Ringstone, which would make it easier to track her down."

"Did the woman tell you where she moved to?"

"No, but I used Linkedin to locate a realtor named Ringstone, and with a few facts—her maiden name, college, and hometown—and using other search sites, found her. She is a real estate agent in Charlottesville, Virginia. Her picture was on the realty website. She's pretty, seemingly unbothered by gray hair and scattered wrinkles on her face. Facebook had more about her. Go ahead and look at the link to see what she looks like. I'm late getting back to school. Love you, Dad. Keep me posted."

"Love you, too, Bethany, and thank you for your research. Drive carefully."

As soon as Alex hung up, his secretary, Lilly, came back into his office. Lilly, a tall, slightly broad-hipped woman in her early sixties, had been working for the insurance agency for fifteen years.

"It was nice talking to Bethany, although she was anxious to talk to you. She hasn't come to the office for three or four years, Merideth even longer."

"You used to give them candy and had toys in the file cabinet. I guess when they lost interest in sweets or playing with dolls, you got bumped," Alex joked. "They both asked about you, wondering what you'll do next. You don't have to quit, you know. The buyer has promised to offer you the same job. Also, thanks for coming in today."

"It's time to retire. My husband already has, and we're planning to move, anyway."

"I'm going to miss this place," Alex said.

"You haven't been quite the same after the divorce, Merideth getting married, and Bethany at college. Will you stay here?"

"I haven't thought that far ahead. The house is too big, as my daughters keep reminding me. Bethany is home on holidays and semester breaks, but she's talking about graduate studies at a university far away. Merry's house is not far, but I'm sure her husband would like them to spend time with his parents, and frankly, she's been cool since Pietrina died. Maybe I'll know after my *quest,* as my youngest child calls it." He'd explained his plans to Lilly.

Later, he packed personal items from his desk. By Friday of the following week, he had made all the arrangements to transfer the business, cleared out his office, contacted his clients, encouraged them to stay with the new organization, and said goodbye to his staff in the office and the field. Lilly was the last person to bid him farewell. They embraced, saying nothing, as if words would unleash the emotions they'd held back since his announcement.

At home the next day, Alex followed up on his daughter's efforts in locating Carolyn Lipinski. First, he entered the name of the realty business, Virginia Homes, and scrolled through the agents' biographies and photos for the region. He found Carolyn and agreed with his daughter's impression: she was attractive, and immediately recognizable as the girl he knew from high school and college. He delayed contacting her, giving himself a few days before calling a woman from his past. He was transferred to Carolyn's line when he dialed the town real estate office.

"Carolyn," he started, "you may not remember me, Alex O'Rourke—"

"Of course I know who you are. We were kids together, and you were my first love. We met years later at a school reunion."

His voice rose. "You do remember."

"You were trim, handsome, and adventurous, although not many people knew. We had a great time together, and I was nuts about you."

"And I about you. When I look back, I remember being awkward, but you helped me change. I was hoping to drive down there and meet you."

"Are you looking to buy a house in the area?"

"No." He hesitated before continuing. "I just thought seeing you and talking about old times would be interesting."

"That's fine with me," the puzzlement apparent in her voice. "We could reminisce. What have you been doing since college? I'm sure you told me at the reunion, but I don't recall."

"I'll explain when we meet."

"You can also explain how you found me."

They planned to get together in two weeks. She gave him her home address and phone number. Until leaving, Alex considered what he would say, wondered how much she remembered their dating and what they would discuss about the years since.

When he arrived at her house early evening, he held his finger inches from the bell for a minute before pressing.

Carolyn stood in the doorway looking at Alex, and he was staring at her. "I never thought I'd see you again; this is such a pleasant surprise."

"For me, too." He answered as she pointed inside.

They stood awkwardly in the living room until they hugged quickly, she initiating.

"I thought we'd go out for dinner," Alex offered. "Name the restaurant."

Carolyn wore a print top, slim, dark pants, and black, low-heeled shoes. Her makeup was light, and her lips were colored with pink lipstick. Her eyes were a deep blue, nearly black, he thought. He was momentarily transformed to a time early in their teenage relationship when he'd arrived at her house to take her out, and he couldn't take his eyes off Carolyn, not hearing her mother greeting him.

She broke the awkward silence, "There is a restaurant in town with an eclectic menu that's popular among residents; reservations aren't necessary. We can take my car."

They mainly chatted about the town and area on the ten-minute drive to the restaurant, saving the questions until they were seated at a table inside. The town consisted of parallel buildings, mostly stores and shops, a small supermarket at one end and a high-domed church at the far end of the central avenue. A few streets branched off, and the restaurant was on one of them. A small man was sweeping the sidewalk in front of the drugstore, and proprietors were pulling their shop doors closed and locking up, a few waving to Carolyn. The restaurant waitstaff recognized her; one man with a soiled white apron greeted Carolyn and signaled to a waiter.

"He's the owner and chef. I helped him find his house," she explained to Alex.

Once seated and after requesting wine from the waiter, Alex said, "You're popular in this town."

"I've been here for quite a few years, and my occupation allows me to meet people. After years of working in metropolitan areas, I enjoy the small-town atmosphere. I've largely lived in what I'd call a suburban community or city after graduating college, which doesn't have the charm of this town or where we grew up. We both have questions, I'm sure. I get to go first. How did you find me?"

Alex laughed. "I have two bright daughters, but my younger helped track you down." He explained how Bethany was able to locate her.

The waiter arrived with the menus, and Alex and Carolyn stopped the discussion to look at the choices. Carolyn signaled, and they gave their preferences to the smiling waiter.

When Carolyn grinned, Alex asked her the reason for the smile. "The waiter's name is Manuel, and if you look at him after you select, he will nod or shake his head as a comment on your pick. He smiled for both our orders—a good sign."

"Why doesn't he just suggest something?"

"Oh no, he thinks that would be presumptuous. I know it's your turn to question, but I'm too curious to wait. Why did you try to find me?"

Alex explained his plan as he'd described it to his daughters, watching her face for any expression that would convey her reaction. Her eyes widened as he offered the reasoning, but she otherwise showed little response.

"So, I'm one of three. Is there any order or common criterion to the women?"

"Only chronological. They, you, were the most important relationships in my life before my marriage."

"Are you still married?" She pulled her head back slightly.

Alex went into a long explanation about his former wife and her recent death.

"I'm sorry." She put her hand over his. "That must have been doubly traumatic: divorce, then death. My marriage didn't last because of my husband's infidelity. He didn't pass away, but we've had no contact since the divorce. I only get updates through my son, even though I don't ask. You mentioned you have two daughters—tell me about them. I know I'm monopolizing the questions, but if you remember, I did most of the talking when we were together."

They both laughed. Alex spoke about his daughters, unconsciously grinning as he described them. She boasted of her son, sharing his academic achievements and professional accomplishments.

The waiter returned with the meals and the bottle of wine Alex had ordered. Periodically putting down their utensils, the questions restarted, beginning with Carolyn.

"When you first came to my house, I had one of those *déjà vu* moments. Do you still use the same cologne you did in high school?"

"Yes," Alex answered, the pitch of his voice rising. "I'm a creature of habit. I remember you used to call it my love potion. Did it work?"

Carolyn blushed and quickly said, "Back then."

Throughout the dinner, they mostly shared history: their careers and marriages.

After they finished, the waiter approached with the dessert menu, but Carolyn looked at Alex. "Let's not; we can have coffee at my house." The waiter walked away with Alex's credit card. Carolyn explained, "I'm curious about this quest of yours. Isn't that what you said your daughters called it, but that's not something to discuss in a crowded restaurant."

They headed back to her house, barely conversing on the way until Alex spoke. "I'm impressed, and perhaps flattered, by your recollections of our relationship from so long ago."

"It was a magical time in my life when we were on the brink of early adulthood, but without the worries and stress that would come. We're not far from my home; we can settle back, have some coffee, and I have an apple pie in the refrigerator. That may not be as tasty as the dessert menu at the restaurant, but it will be much quieter."

As she mentioned, they pulled into her driveway ten minutes later. They entered the house, and Alex looked around the rooms. When he had first showed up at the house to meet Carolyn and go to the restaurant, he hadn't glanced around, keeping his eyes on her. Now, he used the time to look at the furnishings and wall hangings.

"I need to check my messages. I give my clients and other brokers my work and home number." Carolyn said while she listened to her messages, most of which Alex could sense from the scattering of words he heard were business-related.

He thought the rooms were tastefully furnished—the sofa and chairs were made of a light wood with bright-colored cushions. The wall paintings were artists' originals, most in vivid shades against the muted walls.

After finishing the calls, Carolyn went into the kitchen to make coffee and returned to the room with a tray and two steaming cups.

Alex asked, "Which cell number did you give me?"

"You have my personal cell number. I minimize giving out that number to keep the line available. My mother is ill and in a nursing home. I don't want to miss a call from the facility. Also, my son doesn't realize that some phones work by landline, not cell towers."

"I should feel honored."

She handed him a cup with the realty logo embossed on one side; Carolyn sat on one of the chairs. Taking in a deep breath, she said, "I enjoyed seeing you and having dinner, but I want to understand better what you are doing and why you're here. Are you trying to rekindle past relationships and eventually choose one of us? I feel like I'm on the last round of the tv series *The Batchelor.*"

"No, I'm not trying to restart relationships. I know you are divorced; the other two could be happily married, but that wouldn't stop me from contacting them. And what do you mean by the comparison to a television program, one I've not heard about?"

"*The Batchelor* is a program about a handsome man set up with two dozen women and weekly reduces the number until the final three. He has sex with the finalists to consider—you know what I mean."

Alex put the coffee cup on a side table. "Wait a minute! Do you think this is part of a plan to bed women I once knew?"

"No, I think you're looking for a repeat of the past familiarity in a once-important relationship. You've divorced after a long marriage, your ex-wife dies—"

"You don't believe the reasons I gave you for looking up women I was once fond of? Maybe this was a bad idea. I should leave."

"Don't," she pleaded. "Sit down and talk to me. If you still want to go, fine. You have to admit the timing leads in that direction. Since you called, and especially after this evening, I have wondered if two people, you and I, were both available, having shared a special, although immature, love, could have something together at our age. I know the feeling of being divorced, the lack of any new involvement taking root since, and the emptiness compounded by children growing up and leaving. We were also friends when we were kids; we can restart that aspect. Let's try."

Alex didn't respond for a minute. "I've been told to look forward, not backward, and have done so but haven't clicked with the women I've dated since the divorce and Pietrina's death. Maybe by understanding what I had with women in my past, I can better know what I can do in a future relationship. But you must believe I would never treat any involvement with you or the other women as a game or a deception to get you in bed. I would like to spend time with you as a friend and form new memories, and even if we never see each other again after this, I'll have those and the early memories to cherish."

She laughed, which surprised Alex. "That was well-phrased; you would have been a better writer than me."

Alex bit his lower lip and broke out in laughter. "You're right; that was pretty good, also a bit dramatic."

After a glass of wine, Carolyn talked about her marriage and her life. "I was stunned; I thought we had a great relationship when I discovered the affair. It wasn't a fling; he'd been seeing her for over a year. I didn't comprehend how someone you knew so well could be insensitive and untrustworthy, and I was angry at myself for being blind. Larry, my husband, and I had long talks and separated for a while, but we couldn't stay together. He eventually married his former mistress. My son doesn't talk to my ex much and doesn't initiate the calls, which is sad. After Larry left, I didn't know how to start dating again. I wouldn't try for a few years and was frightened of being hurt again."

Alex followed with an explanation of his marriage. "Certainly, my ex-wife's death impacted my life and perhaps was a factor in why I'm doing this, but I didn't want to meditate on my reasoning endlessly. Pietrina and I had a good marriage, but eventually, our relationship changed, and to use a cliché, we grew apart. Before we separated, we met with a marriage counselor, and the woman kept asking what we could do better, which is a polite way of asking what we did wrong. After the sessions, Pietrina and I would talk at home and agreed that no one seems to accept simply that love can diminish to where we were not enough for each other. We understood relationships mature and change, but there still has to be a momentary and unique reaction upon seeing the spouse, needing to touch, and being familiarly intimate, physically and emotionally.

"Of course, the counselor asked about our sex life, and we conveyed we had tried enhancing that part of our marriage, but our feeling toward each other didn't change. Maybe we were old-fashioned, but neither wanted sex without deep love. Songwriters create lyrics about dying love without reason, but people don't accept that notion, absent of purpose or fault. I believe even my daughters don't accept it, especially my older. That's also why I'm not trying to seduce you or anyone else."

They continued talking for hours, mostly answering each other's questions about their marriages.

"Wow," she exclaimed, "this conversation got pretty deep so soon after we reunited. I was concerned we'd be awkward with each other after so many years."

"That's true. I've told you things I've not shared with anyone else. That's a good thing."

She stood and moved closer to him. "As a real estate agent, I have varying work schedules, but I'm off tomorrow and Saturday. I don't know when you plan to move on, but let's spend time together if you're here for those days. No expectations."

"I have no timetable, so I can stay as long as possible. No expectations."

"Good. We're about forty minutes from Charlottesville. The town is pretty and infused with spillover vitality from the University of Virginia campus. There are many places to eat and great wineries scattered about the area. Come here about late morning. You can drive; I'll navigate."

"That sounds fine."

Carolyn moved closer to him and kissed his cheek. "I'm sorry I offended you earlier. You were not deceitful when we were together, and I should never have assumed you had changed."

"On that note, I'll leave and see you tomorrow morning."

Three

Alex returned to the motel and sat on the chair next to a small table. He thought about what Carolyn had said regarding his reasons for seeking former partners. Was it to search for romance with a long-ago lover because of the confusion of all the recent occurrences in his life, or simply a wish to go back in time?

Bethany answered on the second ring. "Hi Dad, how's it going?"

"Great. I had dinner with Carolyn, and we talked about old times."

"Did you *reconnect*?" she asked coyly.

Alex didn't answer but said, "She pressed me on why I'm visiting three ex-lovers, comparing my meeting with women of my past with a tv program, *The Batchelor*."

Bethany laughed. "I love that program! Do you know what happens near the end, which relates to my earlier question?"

"Yes, Carolyn told me, and I'm glad you're having fun with this."

"Sorry, Dad, but you have to realize any one of the three women will have the same question; Merry and I did, too. We thought of the tv program but didn't want to mention it because we were afraid you'd be angry."

"Her questions, which were more a challenge than an inquisition, have been on my mind since; but I was surprised she would think I was replicating the plot of a television show."

"Dad, you have to be prepared for skepticism. If a boyfriend from my past were to suddenly call me, I'd wonder about his motive."

Alex laughed. "You're twenty-one; you don't have a past."

"Very funny. Outside of the probing, how was your time with Carolyn? Has she changed much?"

"When we were kids, she was delightful, fun, bright, and warm. She hasn't changed, except for being more direct and self-assured; of course, we've both changed physically, but she is still an attractive, slender, and energetic woman. It was nice being with her. I should have expected the blunt questions; she was that way in the past—no artifice."

"I'm glad. Are you staying longer?"

"Yes, at least through tomorrow. We'll see after that."

They talked longer, mostly about things going on in her life and her sister's.

In the morning, Alex went to a nearby diner for breakfast. The cloudless sky and the mild temperature held promise for the day. After showering and shaving, he was completing dressing when the room phone rang.

Without greeting, Carolyn blurted, "I can't meet with you today."

"What's going on? You seem upset."

She paused before answering. "I have a client—a sweet old couple, the Teagles—who are moving to Florida. They left a few days ago to house-hunt down there while asking me to continue listing their home here, adding they would like me to check on their residence while they're away. They gave me an exclusive listing, so I felt I should do that. Last night, someone broke in. I'm going over there now. I don't know what was damaged or stolen; the police are at the house. Alex, I like the couple and feel responsible."

"What could you have done differently, stay over there every night? It's not your fault."

"Thanks, but I need to go to the home to see. If I'd gone over there more often, stopped over at night, put lights on, maybe—"

"Carolyn, why don't I go with you? If there is damage or loss, I can record the destruction to help the owners file a claim with their insurance agent. Many people are so upset about a break-in they ignore detail and don't document to facilitate their claim payment. I can do that."

"That's not why you came here. I feel bad about canceling and don't want to put you to work either."

"I don't mind. You could have stopped by the house without having dinner with me. If you feel guilt, so should I."

"Weak logic, O'Rourke, but I could use your help. Afterward, I'll treat you to dinner. Take your car. I may need to stick around longer, but you don't need to stay. Come here first and follow me."

By the time Alex arrived at Carolyn's place, she was coming out the door. He could see the upset on her face.

"I know, I look awful, but I rushed through dressing and applying—"

"You still look great," he responded.

Carolyn got behind the wheel, and as she turned on the ignition, the door on the other side opened, and Alex got in.

"I thought we agreed you'd take your car, too."

"Gas prices are pretty high, so I'll save money by going with you." He was smiling smugly.

"But Alex, it's not that.... Never mind."

As they pulled up to the ranch-style structure, she parked alongside a police car. Stepping out of the vehicle, she looked toward the front of the house and staggered slightly. Alex put his arm around her shoulder to stop her backward motion. The three front windows were shattered.

"Carolyn, the perpetrators have likely done malicious damage. They could have broken a window to get in, but not all three. It could be worse inside. Be prepared."

Her eyes filled. "I can envision how upset the Teagles will be."

When they went inside, they saw two young cops walking through the rooms. Carolyn explained she was the realtor handling the house sale and watching the home while the owners were away. The young police officer looked at Alex.

"I'm an insurance agent," he explained, not offering that he had no connection to the residence or owners.

Carolyn looked around the living room and put her hand over her mouth.

"Ma'am, other rooms look worse," the young officer said.

"Okay, Carolyn, I brought a pad and pen and left them in your car. I'll get them now, and we can record the damage."

"Just don't touch anything; the crime scene specialists will be coming soon," the police officer warned.

Coming back in, Alex began writing while Carolyn went into the main bedroom.

"It was just vicious. The draws were pulled out, but we'll need the owner to determine what's missing. Why is that expression on your face?" she said to Alex when they went back into the living room.

"I hate adding to your upset. Some of the furniture pieces in the living room were expensive antiques."

"Are you sure?" Carolyn asked, biting her lip.

"I've long been interested in antiques, took courses, and read books. I haven't been involved in damage assessment at my company for a long time, but I was asked to look at possible antiques after a fire, flood, or theft." He pointed to a chair with broken legs and added, "That's a valuable piece."

"My God," Carolyn said and turned away from Alex.

"Let's log each vandalized item, write down what was done, and I'll take photos with my cell camera and send them to your phone. I can select the angle to capture the destruction best."

They worked for hours, interrupted by the crime scene investigators taking photos and dusting for prints. Later in the day, the owners called Carolyn, and she summarized the harm done. After ending the call, she looked at Alex.

"I could have used the wine we might have bought in Charlottesville instead of taking inventory of an elderly couple's devastation. I hope you don't mind if I rescind the offer of dinner out. I'm not hungry or good company." She touched his face as she spoke.

"Carolyn, you had no lunch; you must be starving. I'll get us a pizza and a bottle of wine. I saw you had a stack of DVDs so we can watch a sappy movie afterward, and you don't have to say anything the whole night."

"What makes you think I collect DVDs of sappy movies? But it sounds like a great idea."

They drove back to her house, and she gave him directions to the Italian restaurant and nearby liquor store while she set the table. Upon returning at dusk and walking into the dining area, Alex saw that she had placed lit candles on the table and dimmed the room. He put the pizza box in the center of the table and saw Carolyn coming out of the kitchen, frowning.

"I try to create an ambiance, and what do you do, set a pizza box with a clown picture as the centerpiece," she teased.

Picking up the box and taking it into the kitchen, she said, "The opener is at the far corner; please remove the cork. She returned with two plates, each holding a pair of slices."

"Sorry I messed up the atmosphere you were creating, but I'm glad you can make fun of me. It means you're feeling better."

"I'm grateful to you for getting the information to file a claim, but you were also my moral support. Let's agree not to talk about the break-in tonight."

They chatted between bites and sips of wine, mostly about aspects and events of their lives when they were once together. When Carolyn turned her head or took her eyes off Alex, he stared at her. In turn, she glanced at him periodically.

"We never got to Charlottesville; how about tomorrow?" Alex asked.

"That's fine with me; I have the day off. Let's leave at ten instead of twelve. We'll go to touristy spots as well as the wineries."

After eating and cleaning up, they settled on the couch across from the large television mounted on the opposite wall. Alex sorted the DVDs, yanked one near the bottom of the pile, and lifted the film. "Wow, I found *Love Lost and Found*. We saw that together when we were teenagers. Let's watch it now. As I recall, we were sitting in the back row of the theater balcony and missed much of the movie."

"I don't remember that," she said.

"You must have had a reason for buying the DVD." He started singing "Memories like—"

"I'd say, don't quit your day job, but you don't have one. Hey, before we watch it, I'll make some popcorn. Just be a few minutes."

She came back and settled close to Alex so they could watch. Periodically, they looked at each other and said, "Do you remember that scene?" Their faces were inches apart.

Midway through the movie, Alex felt Carolyn's head rest on his shoulder; fifteen minutes later, she was asleep. Even after the film was done, he didn't wake her.

~ * ~

The next day, Alex arrived at her place a little before ten, and Carolyn greeted him in an above-the-knee tan skirt, a yellow blouse, and flat-heeled shoes. The day promised warm, cloudless weather, and she squinted from the sun pouring in through the open door.

"Let's take my car," Alex said, "you can navigate."

They drove to Charlottesville, slowed by the early lunchtime traffic. Carolyn knew of a place that served the town's best bagels and sandwiches. The tables inside were simple metal seats and Formica-topped tables. Barely able to talk while chewing the thick bread, Carolyn removed a brochure from her purse listing local wineries' locations and pointed to their first stop.

The wineries were scattered throughout the region, but not a great distance apart. Along the way, they toured places of historical interest. Despite the busy schedule, they visited many of the wineries on the list, sampled varieties, and headed back to Charlottesville for dinner. Carolyn suggested a restaurant and gave driving instructions to Alex.

"That was enjoyable; I'm glad we stuck to our original plan," Carolyn said as they entered the restaurant. Her face was slightly flushed; his was as well.

"It was great. The area is an alcoholic's paradise," Alex said.

With the meal, Alex ordered a bottle of wine, and they talked about the day, their different thoughts on the wines tasted the attractiveness of the wineries, and the experiences at each. During their conversation, both would touch the other when drawing attention to a specific point. For dessert, they had Irish coffees made with strong liquor. After he paid the check—over her protest—Alex stood, slightly unsteady on his feet.

"Are you okay, Alex?"

"I've had a lot of wine today. I'm feeling it now."

"I'm not much better, and my stomach's upset. I shouldn't have had such a heavy dinner on top of the wine. What should we do?" Carolyn asked.

"I have an idea." He called the waiter over. "Is there a hotel or motel nearby?"

The waiter frowned. "Look around and you'll see the tables are all occupied, and on your way out, you'll notice people waiting. The university has a big event, and the parents have all come here for the celebration. I believe all the accommodations are full, or nearly so. The Robin's Nest motel is just down the street; I'd check there."

Carolyn said nothing until the waiter left. "You want to stay in a motel?"

"We both feel what we consumed today, including at the restaurant." They were standing near the door. "Your house and where I'm staying are a good enough distance from here. It's dark, and look up: black clouds have moved in, and rain is imminent. We'll get two rooms, and I'll pick up the tab."

"Don't you think it will look odd if we check into a hotel without luggage?" Carolyn asked.

Alex thought for a minute. "I filled two suitcases when I left home. After I checked into the motel near you and unpacked, I put the empty cases back in the truck. You can carry one, and I'll take the other."

"You have this worked out pretty well; did you plan it? I agree with your idea, but I'm paying for my room."

The sleepy-eyed desk clerk searched the room list online. "I'm sorry, but I have only one room with two single beds."

The rain started and pinged against the outside awning. Alex and Carolyn looked at each other.

"We'll take it," Alex told the clerk.

Carolyn muttered on the way to the elevator carrying their empty suitcases, "This was a bad idea."

The room was small, as the desk clerk had warned. Alex turned on the table lamp between the beds.

"How's your stomach?" he asked.

"Much better now, but I'm exhausted. It's only ten o'clock, but I'm going to bed. Also, there's only one chair in the room."

"I'm tired, too. I'll join you." As soon as he finished the sentence, his eyes widened. "I didn't mean to imply—"

Carolyn laughed. "I know what you meant. I'm sorry I got a bit grumpy. We had a great day. This side adventure will add to the memories."

Carolyn went into the bathroom, and when she came out, she sat on the edge of the bed.

"I don't want to sleep in my clothes, so turn around while I undress."

Alex grinned. "I've seen you in your underwear."

She glared at him. "That was long ago-we were together then, and I had a young body. Turn around!"

"If we went to the beach, you'd wear something as revealing as your underwear." He was suppressing a laugh while he spoke.

She jumped under the covers and turned away from Alex. "You can get undressed now. Shit, I hate wearing a bra to sleep."

"I've also seen you without—"

"Don't go there."

Alex couldn't contain his laughter. Later, he heard her moving under the cover, and something fall softly to the floor between the beds.

A few hours later, Alex, still awake, turned to look at Carolyn in the half-moon light coming through the curtainless window. Lifting slightly, he put his hand under his chin, smiled, and watched her as she slept until he eventually fell back on the pillow.

~ * ~

Carolyn was up first and hastily dressed, noticing her wrinkled clothing. She was in the bathroom when Alex woke, and he dressed quickly.

"I'm hungry. I had minimal makeup in my purse to put on, and my hair looks like I'd been mildly electrocuted. I might as well have slept in my clothes because I look like I did. In addition, I didn't shower—you get the picture. The bill was paid, so let's slip quietly out."

"Okay, but I'm hungry."

She blew a breath between her lips. "We'll go to my place, and I'll make breakfast after I shower and change. You'll have to remain unkempt a bit longer."

The rain had stopped, and the clouds moved west to harass another county. They spoke little on the way back, each with their separate thoughts. She rushed out of the car in her driveway and left the front door open while Alex was getting out.

"Coffee!" Alex said with feigned desperation. and went into the kitchen and searched the cabinets for the coffee and the pot. Finding the pot but not the coffee grounds, he went upstairs to ask Carolyn. Alex heard the water running in the bathroom and started back down. Before he reached the landing, she came out and rushed into her bedroom wearing a large towel; his eyes followed her. Behind the partially closed door, Carolyn shouted, "What are you doing up here?"

"I was going to ask you where the coffee was."

"Don't bother looking; I'll be right down."

Carolyn was wearing gray slacks and a light sweater when she came out of the bedroom."

He handed her a steaming cup. "I found the coffee."

"What are you grinning about?" she asked. "I think you knew where the coffee was and were trying again to see me naked."

"I'm smiling about the whole wonderful day with a wacky ending. I couldn't have had a better time."

"It *was* a special day. Go sit down. Breakfast will be ready soon."

They sat across from each other, and despite declarations of hunger, both picked at the food. Carolyn reached across the table and ran her fingers against the side of his face. "Your whiskers grow quickly and feel like sandpaper."

"What do you want to do today?" he asked.

"I want to talk to you about that. My cell phone rang while I was in the bedroom getting dressed. The sweet couple whose house was burgled is returning today and should be there within a few hours. Could you go with me to meet them? You could explain the insurance, and I could use you as moral support again. "I'm normally not so needy.""

"Sure. I'll go to the motel, get ready, and return in an hour or so. Are you worried they'll be angry with you?"

"No, worse. They could be *disappointed* in me."

~ * ~

As promised, Alex arrived within an hour. Carolyn was waiting for him, pacing in front of her house. He drove, and she rehearsed what she would say. She was wringing her hands. At the Teagles' residence, Carolyn knocked gently on the door, and a woman's voice called out, "Come in, the door's open."

Carolyn entered the living room and saw Mr. Teagle sitting on a chair, his head in his hands, while his wife stroked his hair.

"I'm so sorry," Carolyn said. "This is my friend, Alex O'Rourke. He is an insurance investigator and helped me inventory everything damaged, which will help when you meet with your claims adjuster."

The elderly man lifted his head. "Don't apologize; it wasn't your fault. Thank you, Mr. O'Rourke, for your help. Some of the furniture means a lot to us and has been in the family for a long time. I contacted someone who can repair the special pieces. Their value will go down, but not to us. The claims representative is coming shortly, and your observations and notes will be of great importance."

"Is there anything else we can do for you?" Carolyn asked.

"No, some neighbors will be coming over to help clean up after the adjuster leaves."

"Okay, but if you have any questions about the cost estimate from your provider, give Carolyn a call, and she can always reach me."

Walking down the front steps, Carolyn took Alex's hand. "There's a park over there," she said, pointing with her free hand. They sat on a bench near the entrance.

"I'm going to stay for the adjuster, so there is little we can do today. I also need to get back and catch up, likely working into the evening. With scheduled appointments for the following days and two closings, there wouldn't be much time to spend with you. The adjuster can give me a ride home."

"I'm sorry to hear that. I have the time but, of course, not the obligations you do."

"Alex, it's more than that. You have a plan and need to stay with it. Who knows what will come of your time with those other women. At first, I was suspicious and critical of your motives, but now I realize there was no agenda, just a curiosity about people you once cared about, as you said. Maybe there are other reasons you may not even recognize in yourself but will discover, eventually."

Alex breathed in deeply. "I'm going to check out and head home. I don't know what to expect going forward, but I didn't expect how much I would enjoy the time with you. It flew by."

They stood, and Carolyn re-grasped his hand, moved closer, and kissed him. Afterward, she turned back to the Teagles' house. Alex called her name. She didn't turn, but waved as she proceeded.

Four

Alex drove along the main street until he stopped in front of the motel where he was staying. After packing, he dropped the key at the front desk, nodding to the clerk, who asked about his stay. Before he pulled out, Alex called his daughter.

Bethany answered her cell. "Dad, where are you?"

"In the motel parking lot; I'm heading home now."

"How was it? Did the experience meet your expectations?"

"Honey, no questions, not now."

"Are you okay, Dad? You don't sound right. I can meet you at the house, and I'll get there before you."

"No, Bethany. I'm tired and need some time."

"All right, but I'm coming down on Saturday—no argument."

"I'll see you then, sweetie."

As soon as she hung up, Bethany called her sister. "Merry, I talked to Dad. He's coming home, and he seems depressed. Can you break away and be there on Saturday so we both can talk to him, cheer him up if I'm right about how he's feeling. I'm sure you're as curious as I am about what happened with the woman he's been with for the last few days."

Merry stammered and offered reasons she couldn't make it.

"He needs us. Why are you hesitant? Sometime—not this weekend—you and I must talk about why you blame him for the divorce. For now, be there for him."

After dark, Alex pulled into his driveway. Throwing his suitcases into the spare room, he went to his bedroom, fell on the bed, and stared at the ceiling. He reached into his pants pocket, took out his cell, scrolled the contacts list, stopped on Carolyn's name, and nearly pressed. Instead, he put the phone on the night table.

Making himself a sandwich and pouring a glass of wine, he went into the living room and put on the television; the volume was so low the voices on the screen could barely be heard.

The following day, he unpacked the suitcases, put clothes in the washer, and went to the post office to get his mail. He retrieved the messages on his recorder and answered some callers. The routine chores took a good part of the day. He called Bethany to ask what she wanted for dinner, and she told him Merry was also coming.

"I'm fine. There's no reason for either of you to disrupt your lives and drive here."

"I'm sorry, but cell service on campus can be spotty. I couldn't hear what you said. We'll see you on Saturday. Chinese takeout is fine."

~ * ~

His daughters arrived that weekend, Bethany first, followed by her older sister. After the greetings, Merry volunteered to make sandwiches for lunch and went into the kitchen. Bethany took advantage of her time with her father to ask, "How come you didn't shave today? That's not like you, Dad."

"Honey, I'm not working anymore, so I don't have to. It's liberating to avoid scraping my face periodically. Don't make anything of it."

"But even on weekends, you shaved. Never mind."

Merry entered the room and announced that lunch was served on the kitchen table. The sisters looked at each other as they sat and bit into the bread and meat. Noticing the stares, Alex said, "I haven't been gone long."

Bethany swallowed her food and put the sandwich back on the plate. "We want to hear all about it."

Merry interjected: "It can't be life-changing. Dad's right; he was away less than a week."

"Let's resolve this quickly. I enjoyed seeing Carolyn, we had a good time, and I left. No great romance, no rekindling—"

"Are you going to see her again?" Merry asked.

"I have no plans to go back."

"Why wouldn't you want to see her another time?" Merry continued.

"Sis, you're pushing our father; why don't we let him give us the details of his time with the woman."

Alex breathed in. "Her name is Carolyn." He explained what had happened, leaving out reference to any physical contact when she had fallen asleep on his shoulder, hand-holding, and the kiss. The daughters asked questions, frequently cutting into his telling with requests for clarification or more detail. As Alex answered, he could sense a difference in their questions, underlying motives, and suspicions. Merry was more skeptical of his responses.

"I hope this was worth the trip you both made. I'm sure you had better plans. How long are you staying?" Alex asked.

Bethany answered. "We're staying overnight unless you've rented our rooms."

"I'll make dinner for us, or better yet, it'll be a family preparation. First, I have to buy food. Keep yourselves busy while I'm at the store." Both young women retreated into their respective bedrooms, unpacked, and washed up in the main bathroom. Bethany came into her sister's room.

Merry said, "Dad got defensive when you called her 'the woman.' I think his feelings toward this Carolyn are more than he lets on."

"What if he cares for her more than he says? Why does that matter to you? He wasn't married to Mom when he went to see Carolyn," Bethany said.

"That's not the issue."

"What is? When they divorced, neither of our parents ever asked us to take sides, but you were much more supportive of Mom and her new husband."

"And you took our father's side."

"That's not true, Merry. I loved them both equally. Maybe I paid more attention to Dad because you were backing away. Also, I lived in the house with him longer than you did, and that's my home when I'm not on campus. You haven't answered my question: why have you been distant from our father?"

Merry's eyes were half-closed, and her lips pressed together before she spoke. "If he'd tried to keep their marriage together, they might still be wed. Mom never said that, but I know her well enough to read what she feels, even if not expressed." Merry paused, "Brian did his best; Dad would have been better for her while she dealt with cancer."

"Did Mom tell you she wanted to continue the marriage? Is it the obligation of the male to keep the marriage intact? Your reasoning is full of assumptions. The only reality is you are hurting Dad, blaming him for things he didn't do. I also asked Mom about the reasons for their divorce, and she didn't fault our father. Maybe you read her better than I did, but that's not enough to be so judgmental. He can sense what you feel about him, that you're holding back."

Just as she was about to answer, Merry's phone rang. Before looking, she said, "It's probably my husband." Her eyes widened. "Hi, Brian." She looked at her sister. "Can I call you back?"

Bethany stormed out.

Alex returned and put the grocery bags on the kitchen table, looking for his daughters as he passed through the rooms. He called their names, and the response came from the bedrooms, leaving him perplexed about why they were there. From his recollection, neither daughter ever took naps nor was fatigued from daytime activities, unless strenuous. Merry was the first to come down the stairs. She always showed upset in her features and posture; she was bothered, he reasoned, and most likely for something involving Bethany.

"Care to tell me what's going on?" he asked.

"Ask Bethany."

"You realize you sound like a child."

"Dad, talking about visiting old girlfriends drags out memories of the divorce, the death..." She stopped to take in a breath. "They all get mixed up. You have every right to meet with women in your past, but the timing—"

"I have a feeling that Bethany doesn't agree."

"I don't know if she sees all these things running together. Most people think I'm the rational, cold person, and Bethany is the more emotional, more caring, but that's not always true."

Alex hugged his older child. "I don't think that, especially about the loss of your mother. Even though we divorced and she remarried, I still loved her, just differently. Honestly, I never consciously considered this timing problematic, but obviously it was. Carolyn asked me why I was going on this 'quest,' as you and your sister named my search. I miss your mother as a friend and you and Bethany, now that you have your own lives. Selfishly, I felt abandoned, and that added to my purpose."

She backed away from her father. "Because Carolyn was so insightful, does that mean you've developed strong feelings toward each other?"

"No, we didn't spend enough time together to develop 'strong feelings,' and I promise that if a serious relationship develops with any of the three women or any other woman, I will tell you and Bethany." His tone lowered. "I regret I didn't spend more time with Carolyn, and maybe that's what you and your sister are picking up on my demeanor. But she encouraged me to continue searching for the others. I don't know if that was insightful, or if she had no interest in spending more time with me. I don't think it's the latter, but I'm not certain."

At that moment, Bethany came into the room. "What's going on?"

"I told Merry I will tell you both if I start a relationship."

Bethany's eyes moved between her father and sibling. She said slowly, "Is that *all* you talked about?"

Merry started to answer, but Alex interjected. "That was the most important."

Alex asked his daughters to set the table at dinner while he prepared the meal. When he brought the sliced meat into the dining room, he saw Merry and Bethany pushing each other softly, both smiling. The light from the picture window darkened prematurely, and heavy clouds dominated the sky. He lit candles at each end of the table, and as he expected, they made a teasing comment.

"How fancy," Bethany said.

Merry quipped, 'Taylor hasn't put candles on the table ever."

"I should have known better," Alex said.

They chatted while eating, and after the meal was done, they put the dishes and utensils in the dishwasher. Merry took the half-filled bottle of wine and the three glasses into the living room. She sat on the couch, and Bethany took the other end. They positioned the other seats across from the sofa. When both looked at him, Alex knew the interrogation was starting again.

"I don't think I put the dishwasher on; I'll go check," Alex said.

Bethany jumped up and said, "You did already; I can hear it. Sit back down and relax. Merry and I have a few more questions."

As if cued, Merry started, "What's next?"

Alex answered, "I have to go shopping for a new—"

"Dad," she dragged the word out. "You know what we're asking. Who's the next victim?"

Alex squinted. "Her name is Madeline—Maddy— Beecham."

Bethany stood with her hands on her hips. "Do we have to apply torture to get more out of you? We want to know what she looked like, what she meant to you, in other words, the history."

Alex took in a deep breath and began. "In the order of your request, Maddy was striking. Her facial features seemed drawn with a sharpened pencil, her eyes perfectly round with green pupils, slightly tan skin, a reflection of her Italian heritage on her mother's side, thin eyebrows, and delicate ears. Maddy had beautiful hair, naturally curly, thick, black, and long enough so she was always throwing her head back to keep the strands from her face."

Merry said, "We got a clear image from the neck up; how about below?"

"If her face was well-chiseled, her body was well-formed. She was slender, which further accented her... you get the picture. She had the smallest feet I'd seen, and I used to tease about how she kept her balance."

Bethany said, "You describe her in such detail more than you offered about Carolyn. Does that mean anything? Have you thought about her over the years?"

"No, only recently. I looked up her picture in the college yearbook."

"Okay, she sounds perfect, so what happened?"

Alex tried to read the tone of her question, but wasn't sure. He described their involvement beginning in the spring semester of his sophomore year and continuing until the senior year. He admitted Maddy ended the relationship, and he never fully understood why. His daughters asked questions, rotating back and forth, and Alex joked they were ganging up on him like a wrestling tag team.

After the inquisition, Merry and Bethany got up from the chairs. Going to the den, Merry sorted through the DVDs. She said, "You haven't added much to the inventory since we left."

"That could be a good thing," Alex said, "you can select the one you enjoyed as a child and see what you think of it as an adult, and it could bring back good memories."

"I have a better way to reminisce." She held up a coverless DVD casing.

Alex knew what it was: a compilation of several videos he had taken when the four of them went on weeklong vacations near their favorite lake.

"Won't watching make you sad?" Alex asked.

Bethany backed up her sister. "But it will be a good sad."

Before the images started, Alex retrieved a box of tissues and placed it between his daughters, who'd settled on the couch. Bethany grabbed the box, waited until her father sat on his favorite chair, and tossed the tissues in his direction. He thought of the irony—a meaningful DVD had been part of his evening with Carolyn and was now another with his daughters.

The images of the sisters in matching bathing suits dipping their feet in the water's edge were followed by their mother holding their hands and slowly bringing them into the water. Alex knew he had done the recording until a later scene showed all four sitting at a wooden table near a grill, the smoke still coming from the charcoal residue. The girls appeared older in subsequent portions, although the background was always the same: the lakefront and surrounding area. Midway through, Bethany got up from the couch, retrieved the tissues, and sat back down, the box in her lap, her thigh pressing against her sister's.

Merry was the first to claim fatigue and headed upstairs. Bethany removed the DVD from the player, kissed her father on the cheek, and went to bed.

~ * ~

In the morning, Alex rose early, and Bethany came down soon after. She poured herself a cup of coffee and sat near her father.

"Dad, how are you going to find number two?"

"You mean Maddy Beecham?" He didn't mask his annoyance.

She formed an exaggerated frown.

"I haven't thought about it much but will tomorrow, starting with Facebook, Linkedin, the usual. I'll deal with the obvious problem—did she marry and change her name? Beyond that, I'm not sure, although I won't hire a private detective or anything like that. There are online services where they can search public records, but I have the same issue—what's her last name? If unsuccessful, I'll just have to move on."

"Can I help? I found Carolyn for you; maybe I can do the same with Maddy."

"Where would you even start? You and your sister have your own lives and obligations. Looking for these women was a long shot to begin with, and largely to satisfy a curiosity. At times, I dismissed the whole effort as a foolish undertaking and should focus on what I'm going to do with my life now that I'm retired. After meeting with Carolyn, I regained my enthusiasm to go through with searching for the others, but I'm not going to search forever, and it shouldn't take too much of your time."

They heard Merry coming down the stairs, fully dressed. "I want to get back early to do some things before the weekend ends." A wide smile formed on her face. "Plus, my husband misses me."

Bethany made a gagging sound.

Merry stuck her tongue out at her sister and filled a cup with coffee. When she finished, Merry announced she was leaving. Alex got up and walked with her to the front door. Before going out, she hugged him and whispered that she loved him. When Alex turned around, he saw Bethany had left the table. He heard the water running in the upstairs bathroom. About an hour later, she came down lugging her suitcase.

"I should be going, too. A lot to do before class." She hugged him and left.

Alex felt like they'd taken the air from the house with them.

~ * ~

Over the next few days, Alex busied himself with chores, playing golf, and responding to questions from the purchaser of his business and former staff members.

One afternoon, he visited the grave of his former wife. He remembered they'd discussed the reasons for the dissolution of the marriage, but always with caution, avoiding blame. There was an increasing wall they could not seem to scale. They'd searched among stock answers: they'd married too early, she needed to do things in her life that she'd once sacrificed, but none seemed sufficient. Their physical intimacy had always been good, but the growing emotional separation had impeded the enjoyment and frequency of sex. After a while, they'd abandoned the effort for an acceptable explanation, and reluctantly and sadly, they'd mutually consented to divorce.

Staring at the settling mound over the grave and the recently added headstone, he remembered that explaining the divorce to their daughters had been the hardest part. Pietrina had seemed happy in her second marriage, content in her late-in-life career, but there was not enough time for her to enjoy the changes; the signs of illness had come to her early in her new life.

~ * ~

The next day, Alex devoted his time to tracking down Maddy, going back to resources like Facebook, where he'd conducted a preliminary search. Beginning with long shots, he canvassed for individuals with her last name in the town where she grew up, hoping to find a relative who knew where she was but without luck. Every other effort failed.

When Bethany called, he mentioned he had been unsuccessful and ended the search for the day.

"Let me help. I know some students who are adept at computer searches. I may not be any more successful than you've been, and I won't duplicate what you've done, but there has got to be some way to track her down."

"Go ahead, but don't spend a lot of time, especially at the expense of things you must do."

"After you two broke up, was Maddy dating someone you know of?"

"No, I don't think so, but I had no interest in following her love life. She ended it, as I told you."

"Did she mention what career she would pursue or any place she would like to move to after graduation? A lot of students don't return home but consider other locations."

"I recall she was obsessed with figuring out what she would do after graduation. Neither of us considered grad school. She would get angry with me because I wasn't focused on my plans. After separating, I needed a long time to get over her, so I avoided Maddy; since we had different majors, we weren't in the same class. I saw her a few times on the grounds, once in the library, but we were both awkward and said hello, but that was about it."

"What was her major?"

"Science, and she got high grades. That major can lead to many directions: medicine, research, and others. It won't help."

"Give me some time," Bethany said, "to brainstorm with my friends. We'll find her, I'm certain."

Alex shrugged. "Thanks, honey," he said.

A week later, he returned from shopping, and after putting away the groceries, he listened to the message on his phone. The voice was his daughter Bethany's. "Call me right away; I know where she is."

Alex dialed her number and could sense Bethany was excited by the pitch of her voice.

"I found her. She married and—"

"Wait! How did you find her?"

"Why is that important; don't you want to know where she is, what she looks like?"

That you've evaded my question concerns me."

Bethany paused. "I'll explain, but don't be upset. I tried everything, but the best source was your college. However, how do I resolve the problem of a name change? College records would not likely list her married name or address. I realized alumni lists would. I called the fund-raising unit, but the person I spoke to wouldn't provide any information. I told you I have friends who are good with computers," she took a deep breath, "and my friend hacked the alumni database. The records were kept by graduation year, and I found a Madeline in that grouping. As you and I suspected, she married after graduation, and like most women, especially in your generation, she took his name. Of course, the file contained her home address and phone number."

"Bethany, what you did was illegal. You could destroy your future if the college discovered what you did, reported you to the police, and the cops could trace the hack to your computer."

"We didn't use our laptops, but a library PC. They don't record who uses them, and we didn't use any identifying sites or passwords. Even if the hacking is traced to the school, they couldn't track the access to my friends or me."

"Bethany, I can't talk to you right now." He hung up and walked the rooms, his face red and his fingers clenching and opening in a semaphore motion.

~ * ~

Bethany cried, and seeking consolation, called Merry. Sniffling, she explained the conversation she'd had with their father and, expecting support, she was taken aback by her sister's response.

"Dad's right—you could have ruined your life. How are you going to start a career with a criminal record? What guy will want to get involved with an ex-con? If you find someone, I can picture the introduction to his family, Mom, Dad, I want you to meet my fiancée; she just finished serving a three-year sentence. Oh, that thing on her ankle is a monitor of her location."

Bethany changed from shock to anger. "You exaggerate. I was hoping you would be on my side."

"Sis, I am, but the thought of what could happen scares me. I blame Dad for this. This hobby of hunting for former girlfriends is a waste of time. He should be thinking about what to do after retirement, like travel, developing a hobby, and date women other than those from his past. Now, he's got you involved, putting you at risk."

"When you and I wanted something, Mom and Dad went along, even if they thought we were being foolish; they considered what it meant to us. This is the same, but in reverse. Whether I agree with the logic of Dad's pursuit or not, it matters to him."

"I see your point."

Bethany said, "Just don't get any ideas about doing the same thing as Dad. If we had to chase around to find every guy you dated—"

"Very funny. I'll calm him down and point out that even if he disagreed with your method, why refuse the results? I'll also remind him how impulsive you are."

Bethany waited a few days before calling her father, hoping he'd cooled and her sister had run interference. Listening to his tone after he'd picked up the receiver, she felt his anger had dissipated.

"Dad, I'm sorry I upset you, but why waste what I uncovered?"

"Your sister said the same thing, which means you two talked. Tell me what you found?"

"Please understand I tried everything: looking for people with the same last name in her former town—no luck. Her sister, the only other child, must have changed her name, too. I was desperate to find her for you. Anyway, her name is Madeline Boughton, she lives in Roxboro, North Carolina, just south of Virginia, and has a Facebook page. She's married. You can get her phone number easily with that information and her husband's first name, Jason. I noticed she differs from your description; her hair is blond, and she's gained weight. However, she is attractive, if that matters. I'll back off now, and you can do what you want."

"I know you intended to help me, but I don't want my interest to harm you. With the information you came up with, I will follow up. But I need you to promise your efforts will not continue, especially in searching for the third woman when I get to that point."

Bethany waited before responding. "I promise, but I may have found former-lover three without much effort and certainly without doing something illegal. I'll talk to you about that after you decide what to do about contacting Madeline Boughton."

Alex hung up, but his mind filled with thoughts of Madeline. Bethany's description heightened his interest in calling and seeing her. Considering the enjoyable time with Carolyn, he should have been encouraged to reach out to Maddy immediately, but he hesitated. While recollecting their relationship, he was still bothered that he hadn't known her reasons for breaking up.

He devised scenarios if he called her: would her husband pick up, and what would Alex say, that his wife was a former girlfriend or maybe mention they went to college together? But it would seem odd to call her after so many years. What if her husband asked how he got their number? He was able to get her home number through online sources, but not her cell.

For two more days, he delayed calling her, but he kept going back to Facebook to look at her image. He had the idea to initiate a friend request. Perhaps from there, he could have a dialogue through Messenger and get a sense of her interest in meeting.

Alex was surprised that within an hour, his request was accepted. Going back to her page, he scrolled down her postings, which included family pictures, some at the various ages of her children, and photos of herself and her husband. As he scanned deeper in the page, he felt as if he were watching her age; some pictures were from the distant past, although recently posted. The one that struck him the most was an old image of their graduation; she was in a cap and gown, standing between her parents, all three with their arms around each other.

Another photo, more recent, showed Maddy beside her husband. He thought it was odd because there was a space between them to the point that part of their shoulders disappeared at the edge of the photo. Their smiles seemed false and quickly flashed for the photograph. Alex speculated about their relationship but dismissed the direction of his thoughts.

The following day, he opened his laptop and went immediately to Facebook. His eyes widened as he saw a note from Maddy. Opening up Messenger, he read her words: *Alex, it's good to hear from you so long after we ended our relationship.* His first response was ire, and he said to himself, "We didn't break up; you dumped me."

When he calmed, he wrote in answer; *A lot has happened, too much to list in Messenger. I've thought about you as well. I would like to meet with you.*

She answered: *My life has also been complicated and too much to describe in the limited space. I looked at your Facebook page—pretty sparse. I guess you're not a big fan of social media, at least for personal stuff. I saw that you have two beautiful daughters and based on your photo, you look good. I suspect you've viewed the pictures on my page and got a glance at me, my husband, and two kids. The best way to communicate, at least at first, is by email. You can tell my age because I use AOL: Maddlady@aol.com (Silly, isn't it).*

Alex read her message multiple times before responding. He'd recognized the relationship with Carolyn had ended because they were young, their capacity to achieve full and mature love unformed, and their ambitions unclear. Too much of their lives was uncertain, and too much time was ahead of them. He considered the same could be said about his relationship with Maddy and their compatibility, but there were distinctive differences. When he was with Carolyn, they spoke of love often; the word came easily and often—too easily, reflecting their youthfulness and ignorance of what the word truly meant. With Maddy, it was different; they used the word infrequently because they understood its significance. His relationship with Carolyn was physical but never consummated—mainly due to lack of opportunity or location rather than deliberate abstaining; with Maddy, the opportunities were available, and they had taken advantage.

~ * ~

His thoughts swirled all day with anticipation and similar hesitancy; eventually, he concluded that beginning the communication through email was an easy first step without commitment. Before starting, he resolved not to make comparisons, to match Maddy against Carolyn. If he avoided Maddy, he would validate his daughters' suspicion about his motive, that he was looking to restart something instead of satisfying curiosity. She was a married woman, and any ulterior motive wasn't present. He envisioned time with Maddy would be pleasant, and he might find out why she dumped him, recalling her *announcement*—he had facetiously called her unilateral decision.

The next day, he emailed her and summarized his life since leaving college, his marriage and divorce, Pietrina's death, his daughters, and retirement, with no mention of tracking down the three women who were central to his life at various times. He knew his first lengthy communication would not be enough detail but hopefully pique her interest. His ploy worked. She sent back emails asking for more information, and he responded somewhat vaguely. The evasiveness shown in their writings led to the next stage— phone calls. Alex offered his home and cell numbers and was curious why she gave him only her cell number. After several exchanges, Alex declared that emails and calls were not enough for two people reminiscing and catching up, coyly suggesting they meet. He was pleased by her willingness. They talked about the timing, and Alex said he would travel to where she was because he had the freedom from work, and she'd have to consider the needs of her occupation, which she mentioned briefly in her email. Alex was enthusiastic about getting together and sensed equal interest in her voice. There was no awkwardness between them when they spoke, and he was convinced there would be no uneasiness when they met.

Part Two

Five

Since leaving Carolyn, he had thought about the past with her and the recent time together, but as the time approached to see Maddy, he tried to put thoughts of his first love aside and not make comparisons. After all, he was not selecting a mate or mimicking a scene from *The Batchelor,* as Carolyn had teased.

The difference was the still nagging question: why had Maddy broken it off? For months after their relationship had ended, he'd wondered where their lives together could have gone, but they were both too young, lacked experience in serious involvements, and had too much of their lives ahead of them.

As much as he speculated about Maddy's choice to end everything, he also pondered whether his reaction then, and perhaps now, was a matter of ego rather than upset over the loss of a future with her. With Maddy, he was open and honest about his feelings, but after her, he was cautious with other women, even Pietrina, at first. With greater opportunity, Alex and Maddy's physical relationship began early. While they were not each other's first sexual experience, the familiarity he felt with her diminished any early awkwardness or anxiousness.

Maddy had rented an apartment off-campus with two women from her year, and with separate bedrooms and a code to warn of entertaining a boyfriend, Maddy and Alex could be together intimately. They took advantage often. Alex giggled at a remembered comment Maddy once made that the three roommates kept a scorecard of who used the code warning of an overnight guest most. Alex and Maddy outscored the other two. But their relationship was more than physical; they shared the college challenges: maintaining grades, putting up with disagreeable roommates, being involved in fraternities and sororities, and going to the many boisterous parties, along with the petty jealousies and flirtations.

~ * ~

In his last phone conversation with Maddy, she'd suggested getting together in two weeks, beginning on a Friday when the school where she worked would be closed for major HVAC repairs. Alex would drive Thursday afternoon, stay at a motel she suggested, and meet on Friday at her house.

He had trouble sleeping the night before he was to leave. Deciding to depart earlier than planned, he arrived in the town near her by mid-afternoon, drove around the area, and, using his GPS, found her house. The home was surrounded by a tended lawn, a garden in the side yard, and cut grass surrounding the structure. Three wood steps led to the porch with chairs scattered about the wood flooring. The door was cherry red with a wreath hung at its center. Tempted to stop and knock, he sped up, deciding to stick to their plans. After driving further, he doubled back to the town and had dinner early at a Mexican restaurant. The foliage showed early signs of fall, and the leaves displayed yellow and pale red edges. The temperature was declining, but he could still be outside in the sun without a sweater or jacket until dark.

Alex woke before dawn, showered, and dressed as the first light appeared on the horizon. He went outside and looked at his car lightly covered with dew, and debated returning home, ending the idea of searching for women in his past, as he'd done before meeting with Carolyn. When he'd first considered the effort, he'd rummaged in boxes piled in the basement for old photographs, hoping to find at least one of each woman. But he remembered that he and Pietrina had severed the past by burning pictures of former relationships. In a euphoric period early in their romance, the symbolic gesture of burning reflected the totality of their love and focus on their future commitment to each other. All his images of the three women were buried in his memory, dulled by time so he could only describe them broadly as he did with his daughters, but not with much specificity. Their social media pictures helped recast their features and illustrate the link between the past and present, but could not capture how they'd changed internally or emotionally. Before he met Pietrina and after the involvements with Carolyn and Maria had ended, he had been tempted for a time to contact both women. That was not true with Maddy; he'd avoided her as much as possible on a relatively small campus, especially while still in college. Among friends, rumors had floated and gossip-filled about the reasons for the breakup, since neither Alex nor Maddy would discuss what had happened. Loyalties were divided, and blame was dispersed, fueled by imagined scenarios. After they'd graduated, Alex and Maddy had gone their separate ways.

Did he want to know why at this point in his life? Did it matter—water under the bridge, according to the cliché? If he had known back then and altered his behavior that pushed her away, could they have mended their relationship if the fault had been his? Would that have changed the trajectory of their lives and all that followed? Alex knew he loved his life after college and his family, but now he pondered: *what if?* He knew with fair certainty that she didn't leave him for someone else. Common friends told him—asked or not—if there was another romance in her life during their remaining college year and immediately beyond. There were too few secrets on the college grounds and nearby student apartments.

Alex found a restaurant in Maddy's town serving breakfast; at the counter, he sipped dark coffee and poked at his eggs until they were too cold to eat. Leaving payment for the meal and a generous tip, he returned the waitress's smile, who glanced at the amount on top of the bill on the table. Alex drove for a while, killing time until eleven o'clock, when they'd arranged to meet at her house. Pulling up at the sidewalk, he got out, walked to the front door, and pushed on the bell. Maddy opened the door and, tilting her head, looked at him for a few seconds before a grin formed.

"It's wonderful to see you. Come in," she took hold of his arm and led Alex into the main room.

Alex had described Maddy as best as he could recall in his discussion with his daughters, remarking that her facial features seemed chiseled, formed in perfect symmetry, and in profile, her pose was the same from each side.

Now her face was rounder and unlike before; instead of two matched sides from the same mold fused, her face was shaped, cheeks lifted higher, her chin in an arc. While he saw her face and body on social media, he couldn't be sure of the recentness of the photo. Her eyes had lost none of their sparkle as if moistened with every blink, and her mouth was still full and sensuous.

Stepping back after the greeting, he avoided looking at her body but could see even from the lower portion of his eyes that she was shapely, and the additional weight gave her frame a fullness. In all of his recollections, Maddy solely wore soft-color lipsticks, but now her face was made up, illustrating her womanliness and graceful aging. The home's interior was a blend of hues and furnishings, so he couldn't define a specific style for the rooms.

She looked at him and said, "Let's not start this reunion with lies. I don't look bad for my age; you look older but are maturely handsome."

"I like that term: maturely handsome," he said, smiling, "but you understate your attractiveness."

"Have a seat." She gestured toward a flowered chair.

He sat slowly and waited for the likely questions, never taking his eyes off her.

"You explained what you were doing, contacting women in your early life, but why?"

"My daughters ask me that, and sometimes I wonder about my motives. It could be simple: satisfying an interest in knowing what happened to women I knew or some deep reason I don't fully understand. I find myself looking up film or TV stars whose fame has passed and those 'whatever happened to' pieces on the internet. This could be a simple curiosity and use of time, which I have more of. Maybe looking you up and others is part of the same curiosity."

"Others? How many people are there, and are all women?"

"Three, and yes, they are. I wanted to contact women I deeply cared for."

"And you don't have the same interest in men you were once close to? You had some good friends back then."

Alex paused before answering. "I've been asked that. No, I never needed to know. Does that seem odd to you?"

"Well, that was your decision. Why don't we chat for a while, and afterward, I'll take you for a tour of the area."

"During our phone conversation, you said you were in education without elaborating. Now, could you explain?"

Maddy explained. "I'm the principal of Leonard Walling High School, named after the town founder."

Alex pulled his head back. "I thought you'd be the CEO of a major business; you were motivated and ambitious."

"I am," she answered "just not as you'd envisioned."

"But you weren't an education major in college."

"I wasn't, but after I graduated, nothing was available to use my major, so I got a job at a daycare center and fell in love with the role. Soon after, I took courses in the evenings and got enough credits, combined with my existing credits, to get an education diploma. After teaching in the lower grades, I went for my master's in education administration, and here I am. Your turn."

Alex described his start in the insurance industry, which eventually led to his own business. "We largely offered medical benefits plans and risk insurance to small and midsize businesses."

"*You* didn't stray far from your degree. I'm not surprised."

They moved on to discussing family, Alex detailing his daughters' lives, avoiding the topic of Pietrina. Maddy talked about her son and daughter, the pride apparent in her tone.

A wall clock chimed twelve times.

"You haven't mentioned your husband," Alex said.

"Nor you your ex-wife. I am sorry about her death. We can keep our discussion light, full of happy remembrance, or stray into the tougher topics. Let's hold off on the latter for now. How long are you staying?"

"My schedule is open since, unlike you, I have no job to go to. I thought this would be a one- or two-day visit, assuming your husband would be home on the weekend. You mentioned he travels, so I understand why you're free today, but not Saturday or Sunday."

"He won't be here those days, but that's part of the longer story. Let's go out to lunch. I know a place that will remind you of our favorite place off-campus."

They took his, since Maddy's car was in the garage and Alex's rental was parked on the street. The drive was short, and Maddy provided the few directions needed. Alex turned without her instruction at one point, which piqued her curiosity.

"How did you know to turn there?"

"I arrived early yesterday and drove around, curious about where you lived. I'm impressed. Many of the insured businesses were scattered, and I drove to some wonderful small towns to meet with clients. I loved those towns, some consisting solely of a row of stores and beautiful surrounding scenery. Your town is charming and the region pretty."

When they pulled up in front of the plain-fronted restaurant, Alex didn't see the connection to their favorite place near the college they'd attended. She watched him for a reaction when she opened the entrance door.

"Brione's," he said in a near shout.

She smiled at his response. "Yes. Isn't it similar to our favorite place for lunch? Many years after graduating, I was at a convention near the college and looked for Brione's—it was gone. Coming here brings back memories."

"Of us?"

She started to answer when a waitress came and led them to a table near the side of the large room. The tables were square, with a chair on each side.

"We never brought anyone to Brione's; it was our place, and we refused to share," Maddy said.

Alex laughed as he sat and took the menu from the waitress's hand. "Everybody on campus knew about Brione's."

"I know, but we always went alone."

Scanning their menus, they lifted their eyes at the same time. "I know what you're having," Maddy said.

"Oh yeah, what?"

"A turkey sandwich on toast, ranch dressing on top, and fries."

Alex thought for a minute and considered changing his planned order, but stayed with his preference—the one she described.

"You were right, but I know what we're both going to order to drink."

Both said at the same time: "Chocolate milkshake."

When the waitress left with their preferences, Maddy said, "If I remember right, you always finished what I left in the glass."

"You were always so weight-conscious, and I didn't see the need to waste good chocolate-flavored milk."

"As you can see," Maddy said, "I've had quite a few milkshakes since."

Alex leaned back and patted his stomach. "I haven't been skimping on sweets. I always thought you were skinny when we were going out; now you look so good."

"I don't recall you complaining about my body in the past, Buster."

The waitress first brought the shakes while the meal was being prepared. Leaning over the glass, he sniffed, drawing in the chocolate aroma.

"You used to do at Brione's, too."

The rest of their lunch arrived. At first, they ate quietly, but Alex put down his sandwich half midway through. "I didn't want to simply see how you've changed physically, share a few memories, and go home. I'd like to know about your life—the good and the troubling times. My youngest, Bethany, calls it obsessive curiosity, especially about people. I'd read a book about a Civil War battle and traveled to the sight of the conflict to get a sense of the place a one-dimensional telling couldn't offer."

Maddy was silent for a while. "I'm thinking about leaving my husband. I don't know why I'm telling you that; we've hardly gotten to know each other as mature adults. Maybe because you've been through a divorce and can advise or discourage me. This place must make me feel like I'm talking to my college sweetheart. Please ignore what I said."

Instinctively, Alex sat erect. "You can't stop there. I want to know. You can't have the relationship we once had without some vestige of caring, some lingering closeness unaltered by time."

"Alex, there's such a positive ambiance here, mostly because of what it reminds me of, especially being with you. Let's wait until we leave."

They finished, and the waitress arrived with the check and shuffled to the front to greet a newly arriving customer. As he placed his credit card on the bill, he looked up at Maddy. The edge of her lips lifted slightly, and her eyes lit up.

"I hope you are a better tipper than you were at Brione's," she said.

"Are you saying I was cheap?"

"Not cheap, judicious."

"I bet you taught English before moving to administration."

When they left the restaurant, she said, "Let's walk. This *is* a pretty town."

They'd walked for about five minutes before Maddy began talking.

"After college, I was focused on getting into public school education. I dated, but the relationships were never serious until I met Peter, my husband. I didn't want to be distracted from my goals in education, so we kept it light for months, seeing each other periodically. It was easy; my husband is a civil engineer specializing in bridges and tunnels, and many of them are nationwide. As a result, he traveled quite a bit and still does.

"Even before we married, I went with him to places across the country, especially during the summer when I was off. With his engineering logic, he suggested I move into his place since he was often gone, and what was the sense of my paying rent for my cramped apartment. I was spending so much time at his apartment, anyway. I was delighted with all that: traveling, living together–when he was home. We had to schedule our wedding around his assignments because he was new in his field and had to broaden his knowledge and reputation."

She smiled ruefully. "The days he was gone were empty, but we spent every moment we could get together when he returned. The projects got bigger and longer, and the locations farther apart, even overseas. He joined another company later, and now he's a partner in the firm. That's why we moved; the business is centered here. The children came, and we both adored our kids. I admit I was upset that raising them took from our time together." She stopped abruptly, "Do you want to hear all this?"

"Yes, I do, unless this is too painful."

"I still don't know why I'm telling you all this, but I'm comfortable with you because we were once close. We discussed everything, with no holding back, no awkwardness. You even knew when I had my period, although I suspected your motive for keeping track," she looked at him with a wide grin.

"For me, the busyness was the excuse to stay away, not the cause of the separation. I didn't travel, but I'd schedule client meetings at night and on weekends. But we're talking about you; don't stop, please," Alex said.

"He was gone a lot, so it was mostly the three of us. My kids attended the high school where I'm principal, and I took them to school and often home. Sometimes they tried to hide the fact their mother was principal. Both are out of the house, and I'm dealing with the empty nest problem, worsened by sensing their presence in the school halls and classrooms like some haunting spirit. I thought I'd retire in a few years, and Peter could slow down, not take on projects for such long periods, but he isn't willing, and I'm spending time alone."

"Have you discussed the problem with anyone or sought counseling?"

"If my daughter were to get serious with an engineer, I'd advise her to run. If Peter is a good example, they take on every problem, like a construction or repair challenge, with a solution based on logic and meticulous planning. He doesn't get it we're dealing with an emotional issue not following a pattern. He dismissed the idea of counseling, but our issue has no systematic resolution or restoration. Marriages aren't bridges. Peter doesn't get that—he doesn't believe in psychologists."

Alex could sense her upset was building as she spoke. He touched her arm and said, "You asked if I wanted to hear about this, but do you still want to keep talking about the problems with your husband?"

Maddy turned, smiled, and took a step closer. "You know I'm unsettled now. That was an aspect of our relationship: you recognized my moods."

"It was easy—your face and your voice reveal your emotions. I wasn't like that. If I was down or had something on my mind, you had to push to get me to open up relentlessly at times."

"That's true. We laughed and cried a lot together."

"*You* cried."

Maddy tilted her head. "Do you want me to give examples of when you bawled?"

"That won't be necessary."

They returned to discussing the past, focusing on the lighter side of their relationship. Turning around, they headed back to his car. When near his vehicle, Maddy said, "We loved each other, didn't we?"

Alex nodded. As he pulled out, he asked, "You said I knew your moods *most of the time*. What did you mean by that?"

She said, "That's a topic for another time. I wasn't sure how long you were staying, and I have to pull together a report for a big meeting with the district superintendent. I'm nearly finished but need to devote more time. Could you drop me off at the school? I'll take you for a brief tour, after which you can head back to your motel and come back here to pick me up at about five. We'll go to my house, and I'll prepare dinner with your help. Let's see what culinary helping skills you've developed."

Entering the building, Maddy took him through the long hallway, passing closed classroom doors, and they went into her office. "I'm sure the building is like the high school you attended; they all look alike, except for one section." They walked toward the rear of the school and through two closed doors into a large assembly room with a stage that could compete with a small theater. Smiling, she took him up a flight of stairs that led to the stage level, and they looked out at the row of fixed seats.

"The high school has the best performance programs in the state: dance, singing, and acting. Several students go to the finest colleges in the country to develop their talents."

"Are you living vicariously through your students?"

Maddy laughed. "I couldn't carry a tune when we were together and less so now. Students display interest in their subjects; some even enjoy the courses and excel in the classroom, but when they get on this stage, they light up and show the talent they didn't realize they had. Introverts come out of their shells, and extroverts find an outlet for their need to entertain and be in the spotlight."

"Wow," Alex said.

"Impressed?"

"Yes, with you: the look on your face and the sense of pride in your tone. *You* light up and glow. I liked what I did for a living, but I wish I'd felt that same joy in my job."

She smiled and touched his arm. "This would be hard to give up," she said as she swept across the room with her outstretched hand, "but this is only part of the job, and other aspects are challenging, difficult, and even tragic. But as much as I enjoy the programs performed on this stage, I am delighted when I see seniors march across from one end to the other with their diplomas in hand." She turned toward him. "You and I were so focused on ourselves, on each other, that everything was secondary. I've since learned that the source of true fulfillment also comes from other places."

"When did you come to that realization?"

"Not long after my career in education started. It was consolation for *our* lost relationship. As time went on, I wondered where our involvement would have led. Maybe because my marriage is troubled, my thoughts are filled with the 'what ifs,' especially after you called. But if we had stayed together, I would have had a different job in a different location, and none of what you see here."

"So, coming here today was to make a point."

"I wouldn't say it was a plan, or I contrived a scenario to bring you here, but on the drive, I realized my working here, my career, has a link to our past. I know approaching the topic would lead to the question I suspect you will bring up: why did I end what we had? I will explain, at least, the reason I once believed. For a little while, let's just enjoy the wonderful memories. I promise I will answer that question before you leave."

"I can wait. See you at five."

On the drive back to the hotel, Alex reviewed what they'd discussed. There was much more to understand—about her life and their long-passed relationship. He lied in word and tone: he couldn't wait, and some things she said had piqued his interest further. He remembered it had taken a long time to get over her, especially considering the abrupt ending. The memories were dust-covered, but the past hurt was vivid. Did he want to hear about his failings those many years ago? Equally, would he want to know that she later regretted her decision?

Arriving a few minutes late, he pulled up in front of the school; Maddy was standing on the entrance steps. "I thought you forgot or decided you'd had enough and went home."

"No way; you promised dinner."

Returning to her house, he was in the living room when she turned to him, "That's not fair. You changed clothes and look good while I'm wrinkled and with makeup that has largely disappeared. Give me a few minutes to freshen up. In the meantime, open the bottle of wine you brought. The opener is in the drawer near the sink." When she returned to the kitchen, she saw Alex had poured into two wine glasses and held them in his hands, waiting for her to return. She had changed and was wearing dark slacks and a pale orange blouse, and, he noticed, Maddy was barefoot.

"Forgot something?" he asked, looking at her feet.

"I never wore shoes in the house. You should remember that."

"I don't recall looking at your feet." He was staring into her eyes.

Maddy blushed. "I'm making chicken parmigiana. How about you prepare the salad and later boil the noodles? First, let's toast a wonderful reunion." She lightly bumped her glass against his.

Alex took the head of lettuce from the refrigerator, along with a cucumber and a tomato, cut the lettuce and cucumber, and sliced the tomato into eighths, adding croutons from the pantry.

She leaned toward him and said, "That's pretty good. I thought you'd simply rip off sections of the lettuce and dump them in the bowls. I'm impressed—for an amateur."

Maddy had prepared the chicken, covered it with cheese, and poured tomato sauce over the poultry.

"The chicken will take a while to cook, so why don't we go back into the living room for a while."

Alex sat on the end of the sofa, placed his wineglass on the coffee table, and picked up a framed photograph on the end of the table. "I assume this is your family," he said as he looked at the picture of a tall man, a young woman, and an even younger man on either side. Maddy was at the end, and all were smiling.

"Yes, my husband and our two kids, although the word hardly fits our children; they are young adults."

Alex took out a photograph and handed it to her. "The oldest, Merideth, is on the left, and Bethany, the younger, is on the right."

Maddy put her glass down, put her arm on top of the couch, and said, "Could you describe your wife, if it's not insensitive to ask?"

"Pietrina was attractive, dark-haired—"

"No, no—those are her general features. Tell me the color of her eyes and hair, the shape of her face, if she was slender or voluptuous. Tell me about her personality. If I'm being honest, I want to picture her, understand what she was like, maybe secretly want to know if she was like me or different."

Alex described his former wife in detail, leaving out the erosion of her features from the disease but concentrating on the woman he knew early in their lives. Maddy lifted her hand to stop him.

"I'm so sorry I asked; forgive me. I can see from your expression that this is difficult. I've been fortunate. Everyone who has been dear to me has not passed on. My parents are elderly but still active, and my siblings are fine. Still, I should have realized my probing was a mistake. For a while, after our relationship ended, I wondered about the person who would capture your heart. It was once a natural interest, but now, looking at you, I realize it's wrong to ask."

He started to talk, and again, she stopped him. "Let's move on to something else. I just heard the ding from my oven that the chicken is done. Let's go back to the kitchen."

They both went back to the preparations. Once in the kitchen, Maddy opened the oven door and poked a chicken piece.

"It's not done. I also realized I hadn't started the spaghetti. I put the burner on high, and the water should be boiling in a bit. The uncooked pasta is your fault; you were supposed to be in charge."

"Hey, I made the salad and bought the wine."

They both laughed at the teasing. Soon the bubbles formed on the top of the pot. Maddy put on the oven light to check the chicken. Turning back toward Alex, she saw him grasp the spaghetti at both ends as if to break the strands before cooking.

"No, no," she said, "you never break the spaghetti in front of someone with Italian parentage. Have you been served broken strands at an Italian restaurant?" She slapped his arm lightly. "There would be a curse on my house; my mother would rise from the dead in protest."

"Pietrina was Italian," Alex said. "I should have known." He was looking at a far wall.

Maddy put her hand over his. "I'm sorry."

The phone rang, and she asked him to watch the stove while she answered. Lifting the receiver, she said hello and walked into the back bedroom, looking at Alex for a second.

Upon returning and noticing the spaghetti noodles were intact, she smiled at Alex. Maddy put the chicken and sauce-drenched spaghetti on plates, and they sat at the dining room table. The scent of tomato sauce and garlic powder sprinkled on the meal followed them into the room. They chatted while they ate, savoring the meal they'd made together. They reminisced about meals they'd cooked at her apartment off-campus, most being a disaster.

During the conversation, she switched the topic. "What's your most vivid recollection of our time together?" After they finished eating, they paused, and she guessed the reason for his stare—the avoided topic.

He moved his head slightly sideways and, after a moment, said, "We were at a motel in New England like so many tourists who travel there in the fall to view the scenery. After dinner, we went to our room, made love, and fell asleep.

"I was up first in the morning, and you were still fast asleep, not waking until after I'd finished showering. I was standing beside the bed when you sat up. You were wearing a blue, short nightgown. For a moment, you and I looked at each other; you were beautiful, even half-asleep, and I realized how much I loved you.

"The sun was coming through the half-closed blinds. I walked to the window and opened them fully. You squinted and tossed a pillow at me. I removed my robe and got back in bed beside you. At that moment, you removed your nightgown, and we hugged so tightly I felt our bodies were fused. The need to be together, to touch so close, unencumbered by clothes, was overpowering; it was desperation, not lust. I don't recall how long we stayed that way, not moving. It was a special time when everything around you disappeared, and you feel a moment of perfection—one of the images that stay with you, blurred over time but never lost."

"I remember; we got up because I had to pee."

He laughed. "I guess we know who's the romantic if I can recall the sweet scene, and you only remember the need to piss."

"Speaking of bodies, I remember when you were into art, bought supplies for your new hobby, and once you convinced me to pose naked. After an hour of staring at me, I jumped up and looked at your canvas—you hadn't even drawn a single line."

"I couldn't draw a straight line, but you fell for it."

Maddy looked at him. "I know it's time to ask."

"Why did you end the relationship?"

"You were a great boyfriend, but we were never tested to see how strong our relationship was, how it would survive a challenge. In the last school year, I had anxiety about leaving the cocoon of college, getting my first full-time job, and starting a career I erroneously thought would unchangeably determine what I'd be doing my whole life.

"I turned to many people for advice and support—my family, friends, and teachers; one day I realized, where was my boyfriend? As you called it then, you were on your last run at freedom, squeezing as much enjoyment as possible, attending parties, getting drunk. I enjoyed those times, too, but when the drinking and laughter stopped, I needed you to simply listen, be sympathetic, or help me sort through the alternatives. You weren't there.

"At that point, I recognized I'd grown past the need to shelter in college life, and maybe you. When I explained my thoughts about our relationship and our future, you were dismissive and laughed it off, claiming I was being too serious before it was time. 'We'll work it all out soon,' you kept saying. You should have known how I was afraid of uncertainty and needed a plan of sorts. I felt you should have seen it coming, but didn't; that was the core problem. I thought you didn't love me enough, or our relationship in that setting was great, but was not enough to continue. I asked you how we would stay together after college, but you didn't want to focus on it. It was a confusing period for me."

"Did you ever sit me down and bluntly say I wasn't being supportive and didn't love you enough to want to build a future together?" Alex asked. "Did you ever tell me you had thoughts of ending?"

"I think that was the hardest part then; I felt I shouldn't have had to. We knew each other so well, instinctively recognized when the other was unhappy or troubled, but at a critical time, you couldn't see what was most often on my mind. I tied your ignorance to immaturity, being oblivious. It was the first time I doubted us and began questioning our lives together. I couldn't tell you I had thoughts of leaving you. Those words would damage our love irreparably, even if we tried afterward."

"You didn't give me a chance to apologize, swear I'd change, or reassure you I wanted us to continue. Perhaps I was oblivious, dismissive, and focused more on myself sometimes, but I wasn't insensitive when it came to you. I would have done anything to salvage our relationship if I had known. You were wrong."

"I know, and for a long time after, I wondered if I'd made the right decision. I was frightened. I loved you, Alex, and there were parts of you I sought in others but never found, even in the man I married. I realized I had made a mistake, and was too hasty, but the chance to fix things had passed." Tears dripped from her eyes. "Please tell me what you're thinking."

Alex released a puff of air. "I need to process and to do so alone." He stood. "I'm leaving now. It would be hard to switch back to recounting good memories."

"I would understand if you went home now and did not want to see me again. I hurt you in the past and likely now. If you want to spend time together tomorrow, call me."

She grabbed his arm, turned him around, and hugged him at the door.

Maddy stayed up late, watching television, not paying attention to what was on the screen. Near midnight, the phone rang. Maddy hurried to grab the receiver.

"I thought about nothing else but what you said. I realized so much time has gone by, our lives have been full, and we've changed. I don't know how our relationship would have gone had we stayed together, but why should the mistakes we made early in our lives spoil the few days with you now? I hope today has meant something to you."

"It did, Alex, very much."

"Let's not talk about that part of our past again."

"Deal, and I have thoughts about what we can do tomorrow, or I should say today. Dress casually. There's a lake not far from my house. We can rent bicycles, and I'll bring lunch for us. The weather is forecasted to be clear and mild. I'm glad you called; come here about nine-thirty. I am looking forward to seeing you."

~ * ~

Alex arrived when she suggested. He was wearing jeans, a long-sleeve shirt, and sockless dockers. Alex looked at her as she opened the door and saw she was dressed in mid-thigh shorts, a dark green blouse, and sneakers. He stepped inside, and she kissed him on the cheek, her lips barely missing the edge of his mouth. At first, he considered her affection was misaimed, and an inch or so further right would have showed a different intent, a signal. He speculated later the kiss was symbolic of her intent, not quite casual but not amorous.

"I took my car out of the garage; you shouldn't be the sole driver."

She got behind the wheel, and he entered on the passenger side. He was drawn back in time to when they'd ridden together, sitting so close he'd barely had room to turn the wheel. Maddy would smile at him, and he'd touch her thigh. The car windows had been open in warm weather, and her hair had blown across her face.

One time, he remembered they were arguing, her hands were in motion as she gesticulated while she was driving, and the car had strayed from the highway lines until she'd almost collided with a truck going the other way. "Pull over," he'd shouted. When he reprimanded her, she'd leaned over, put her hand on the back of his head, and kissed him. Alex was surprised how recollections came flooding out by being near her.

Maddy parked in the lot near the lake. A high mound and scattered trees blocked the view of the water. The weather report was accurate: the sun was the sole occupant of the sky, the early morning breeze had diminished, and the air was warm, potentially rising to unseasonable heat.

The rental bicycles were chained to a rack outside of a small building. An old man sat outside of the structure, waiting for renters. Alex offered to pay for the two bicycles, but Maddy insisted she'd handle the cost.

Awkwardly peddling, they both wobbled down the stone path leading to the trail skirting the lake; quickly gaining control, they bicycled at a steady speed. Riding behind Maddy, Alex watched her legs pumping the pedals, her muscles tightening with each stroke. The concrete path swerved away from the lake and ascended into a woody area where trees hung over the path and covered the concrete with their shadows. Maddy stopped, and her feet were on the ground. Alex drew alongside.

He asked, "You okay?"

"Yes. I love this part of the trail where the sound of people sitting near the water and cars arriving and leaving is blocked out by tree trunks, and even the sunlight has to wind through the branches and leaves. It's the most peaceful place I could ever find." She turned her head slightly, and her eyes were half-closed. She said, "I never took my husband here." Switching from reflecting to joking, she added, "I'll race you for the next quarter mile." Before Alex had time to accept the challenge, she was pedaling furiously.

The road cleared the trees and circled back to the lake until they reached the area where people were assembled.

"There's a spot over there where we can spread the blanket."

They walked their bikes to a segment of grass where few families had staked out. He helped unfurl the blanket and spread it across the flattened grass. Dropping on the hard ground, little softened by the cotton blanket, Alex blew out his circle-formed lips. "Whew! That was a great ride."

Maddy was leaning back, her head resting on her hands. "I used to bike often and take my kids, but it's been a long time since we were here, and for a while, I lost interest." She flipped onto her stomach and looked at him. Alex turned toward her.

"So, how do I compare to number one?"

Alex squinted as he thought about the meaning of her question. "Oh no, I'm not making comparisons. You are two different people, and I'm not keeping a list. My relationship early in our lives, Carolyn's and mine, was typical of teenagers, our emotions not fully developed, our intimacy limited, and the future was distant. More recently, she is mature, grounded, still pretty, and has the same early years' charm. You were a few years older than she when I met you, and *we* were slightly more mature, independent of family, had much more freedom to enjoy the intimacy of our relationship, and the future—life after school—was closer. You are attractive, and I enjoy your company very much."

"Also, I wouldn't define our 'intimacy' as limited," she teased.

He turned his head slightly, but kept his eyes on her.

"Alex," she paused. "What would you have done if she or I were sickly, maybe even dying? Would you still have come? I'm sure you have a youthful image of all of us in your mind; what if we weren't that way and all those early recollections of how we looked and acted were spoiled by reality? Sometimes, we are better off leaving the past where it rests in our mind."

"I thought about that. Facebook images can provide an answer, but photos can be from years before being posted, and illnesses come on quickly with age. But the speculation never deterred me, and for two out of three, I've been right—it was worth it."

"You repeated the dreaded word: 'mature.'" She bit her lower lip. "As principal, I must display maturity, sensibility, and authority. One day, I'd like to walk into the school in a mini-skirt and halter top, prank the head of the board of education, and write graffiti on the walls in the main section of the building."

Alex laughed. "Do you even own a mini-skirt?"

"That's not the point. Didn't you ever want to go to work in a Hawaiian shirt, pink shorts, and flip-flops? You did crazier things in college."

"No, I didn't. Don't forget—I had three females in my house, and they would have blocked the door."

"The prankster of my youth has grown up—how sad," Maddy said.

She took lunch from the basket she'd brought from home, handing him a peanut butter and jelly sandwich and bottled water. "That was a favorite lunch."

"To save money. I've avoided that combination since college. I'll eat it for old times' sake."

They ate in silence until he asked, "Why so quiet?"

She put down her lunch, looked at him for a moment, and began to cry.

Alex's forehead furrowed. "Maddy, what's the matter?"

"I'm so sorry I hurt you. Being with you and seeing you brought back a long, lingering sorrow after I left you and graduated. For years after we were no longer together, I was haunted by so many memories I should have considered before judging you.

"Do you remember when my mother died? We weren't going out long, but you knew I was devastated by the loss. I called you right after I heard, and you came running to my apartment, stayed with me that night, drove me home for the funeral, and remained by my side for everything: the grieving, the wake, and the burial. How could a man who was so caring be insensitive to my concerns in that final year of college?

"I was foolish and judgmental. If I'd looked back to that time and others, I wouldn't have been so hasty." The tears flowed heavily. "I can still see your face when I broke up with you; you were stunned and in pain."

Alex leaned toward Maddy, and her head rested on his shoulder.

"Since you revealed why you left me, I've had time to think, and while I appreciate your remembering the time your mother died, I was insensitive, focusing on filling the remaining college years with parties, alcohol and fun things, avoiding thoughts of the future and dismissing your apprehensions."

Maddy sat up. "I'd didn't mean to bring us down. We had so many moments. I remember when we were in the student lounge, the weak rays of the twilight sun came through the windows on one side of the room. Outside, a light layer of snow was left from a recent storm. We were both taking a literature course, and you were leaning against me reading a paperback of poetry as I was too—I don't believe it was the same book. I'm reminded of that line from a Simon and Garfunkel song where she was reading Emily Dickenson, and he Robert Frost."

"But you enjoyed reading poetry, and I hated it—too obscure."

"Perhaps that was why we chose our different professions. Do you remember when we used to rent a rowboat and go out on the lake near the college? There's a place like that further in this direction," she said, pointing, "where we can do the same. I'm sure your biceps haven't become so flabby that you can't handle the oars."

"You're turning an invitation into a dare."

They walked around the lake to a section where fewer families were located. The trees were set closer to the lake's edge than in the populated area, and the color of the water was a deeper shade. Minor waves slapped the moist dirt, unlike the more placid ends of the other sections.

Rowboats, each with a painted number, were lined up, bobbing gently, anchored by rope to a deck built into the wet ground. On the lake, a few couples were awkwardly poking the water with the flat edge of their oars, lifting unevenly and steering haphazardly, evoking laughter from the rowers. A man rowed more confidently, his children sitting at the back end watching their father stroke. A young couple guffawed at their oars clumsily coming out of the water and splashing them both.

Alex was reminded of his outings with Maddy when they expressed infatuation similar to the lovers.

He paid the attendant, and they took a boat from its mooring, and Alex stepped in first; once settled, he held his hand out to help Maddy get in as the boat swayed. She sat at the broader end of the boat while he sat in the center slab, reached toward the oarlocks, and grabbed the oar handles. Maddy watched him struggle to move away from the tied-up boats and head to the deeper section of the lake. His left oar slapped the water and rose high while the other was immobile. The boat swung toward the active rowing and started to circle until he dug the other oar into the lake. He got both oars moving, but they were not in sync, and they proceeded in an uneven line; Maddy suppressed a laugh watching Alex struggle.

After about ten minutes of shifting directions, he said, "When we would do this at college, you'd sit alongside me, and we would row together."

She squatted, inched slowly toward the center, and settled beside him, taking the oar from his hand. The boat straightened, and after a few strokes, they glided across the water. The center of the seat was narrow, and their thighs touched, although their upper bodies leaned away as they turned the oars. Soon they were passing the other boats and heading toward the lake's center.

"Let's take a break," Alex suggested. Maddy nodded.

"When we went rowing, we often did the same thing: stop mid-lake and just talk."

"I remember one time we argued on the water, and we were both gesturing to the point the boat rocked, and we nearly tipped over."

"You slapped the water with your oar and drenched me. Did we fight a lot?"

"I think when you're in an emotional and intense relationship, the fervency can lead to arguments and jealousies exacerbated by immaturity," Maddy answered.

"I was jealous at times, jealous of the attention you drew from male students and instructors because of your beauty, jealous of the preoccupations in your life that took away time I could be with you."

"You were handsome, and there were girls who'd look at you fondly. I would draw pictures of them with exaggerated features: a big nose, ears like an elephant, or a mouth full of missing teeth. God, that was like high school."

"I never saw those stares or, if I did, I dismissed them. I wasn't interested."

The boat rocked a bit, and Alex suggested they row back to the shore. By the time they were near the lake's edge, their strokes were smooth, and their oars lifted and entered the water simultaneously.

The attendant grabbed the tossed rope in the front of the boat and yanked them to the wood dock. Alex stepped out of the boat first, extended his hand to her, held her hand as they got out, and walked across the grass. Maddy released Alex's hand and waved to a woman a short distance in front of them. They rode back to where they'd rented the bikes, and Alex took them back to the rental building while Maddy folded the blanket, picked up the basket, and put them away.

In the car, he said, "I'm getting hungry; any restaurant suggestions?"

"Yes," she answered, "but I first want to go home and freshen up, even take a quick shower. You can use my kids' bathroom to wash up, unless you want to go back to the motel first."

At her house, she excused herself after pointing toward the other bathroom. Alex was done quickly and went back into the living room. From where he stood, he could hear the shower running in her bathroom, the flow of water bouncing off her body. He circled the room, unable to settle on a chair. Maddy came into the room, her hair still moist, her makeup recently applied, and wearing a change of clothes.

"This place is not fancy, but the food is great," Maddy said.

The restaurant was near to Maddy's house. Alex parked out front, and they entered the wide door. Inside, the tables were scattered about in no order—a long counter with stools was to the right. A waiter greeted them at the door, took them to a table near the south-facing window, and placed a menu where they were to sit. Both looked at the laminated menu and quickly decided what they wanted. As Maddy had said, the place offered simple fare. The waiter took their orders and shuffled to the kitchen behind swinging doors.

Before the meal arrived, Alex said, "When we talked yesterday, you spoke of the issues with your husband, but we stopped because you were getting upset. Is there anything you want to talk about now?"

"I don't think our situation is unique. We were happy, like most couples at the early stages of their relationship. Our separate careers were our major preoccupation during the week, sometimes spilling over to the weekend. The children came, and our time after work, and on most weekends, had a new focus. And our life continued that way until our children went to college and, soon after, moved out.

"When it was just the two of us, we were almost awkward with each other. I don't know what happened. We had a life together before we were married; why not after the children left? I'm jealous of Peter's job and the sense of being second to his career.

"I know there is a core of incompatibility in most relationships that early in marriage is obscured by the newness, the expectations, and the sex. Routine is anathema, and the differences come to the forefront and are pronounced and spotlighted. My best friend, with whom I shared my feelings, called me a coward. She knew I'd talked to Peter, but she advised me to elevate, to issue an ultimatum."

"Is she still your best friend?"

"Less so. Ironically, I'm facing another challenging time, and my husband is not there for me, but you are."

The waiter arrived, and they stopped the conversation until he was far away.

Between bites, she continued. "My job is challenging, but tiring. I hear the word 'burnout' too often in my field and have been dismissive of the concept, but now I better understand you can reach a point where a profession you've always loved can be fatiguing and eat into your motivation. It irks me that some people think teaching and being a principal are nine-to-five jobs, and we have summers off. I've become hardened in my job and my marriage. The benefits are great, especially the pension. Fortunately, I've been in this job long enough to retire, and at my age, I have the energy to take on new challenges and see places I've only thought about. Perhaps there will eventually be a time when even those interests diminish, and comfort and familiarity become important. I want to enjoy an unencumbered life, love deeply, fully, as I once loved Peter," she paused, "as I once loved you. That's selfish, I know."

"I don't think so, and there are parallels to my life and my marriage, but Pietrina and I came to a conclusion about our relationship at pretty much the same time. I suspect it's not the same for you and Peter."

"Alex, did you ever cheat on your wife between the time you realized the marriage was ending and the divorce?"

"No, I can't give you a reason, but I never considered it. Why, have you thought about it?"

"A man who sold supplies to the school invited me to lunch. He was careful not to risk the business but subtly conveyed an interest in getting together again."

"Were you tempted?"

"Yes, he was good-looking and single." She paused and laughed. "And at least ten years younger. I let the hint pass." Maddy sat up straight in her chair. "My problem will not be resolved now, so let's not talk about failing relationships, separation, or divorce."

"Okay, so what can we do tomorrow?"

Her face brightened. "I found something we'd never done in college—go to a county fair. The event is what you'd envision or see on television. We'll have fun. Each year, the fair has carnival-like activities: rides, prize-winning challenges, fast food, and cotton candy. After that, it will be a surprise."

Alex paid the bill, and they walked to the car, but Maddy stopped as she reached for the handle.

"Let's walk around town," she said.

The sidewalk ran past shops and businesses on both sides of the street. Some stores were closing, and the proprietors removed items from the window or out front. A man in a stained apron was carrying a garbage bag to the back of the store. In front of a dress shop, a woman was sweeping the sidewalk, humming while pushing dirt and debris into the roadway.

The sun was at the horizon, and street lamps flickered, building to full illumination once darkness came. They strolled mostly in silence, and Alex noticed Maddy walked closer to him than times before, so close he could smell the lemon scent on her skin. At times, her motion slowed, and she looked toward him, as if to about to say something, but held back and quickened her pace.

Afterward, Alex pulled into her driveway. Her cell phone rang, and she didn't pick up.

Looking at the message, she said, "It was my son. I'll call him back later."

"I thought it might have been—"

"No, my husband won't call until midweek. He's predictable."

"How do you think he would react to you being seen with me in town or the lake and driving you home?"

"I'm not sure. He's never been the jealous type. I don't know if I should be flattered or insulted."

They got out of the car and walked to her door. "Alex, I'd invite you in, but I'm tired, and we have a full day tomorrow."

"The fair and a surprise."

Maddy kissed him softly and walked inside.

~ * ~

In the morning, Alex arrived, and Maddy was waiting in front of her house. "You're early," she said. She was dressed in jeans and a cotton shirt and was carrying a light jacket over her arm. Her hair was pulled back in a ponytail.

"You kept your hair like that often in college."

"I wore little makeup and simple hairstyles like most girls too lazy or hungover to spend time with preparation. I haven't used this style much since."

"I'm glad you did now."

The fairground was a flat stretch of land with games, rides, and scattered tents. A crowd had already formed at the entrance, and a sweating attendant gathered the admission cost and handed a sticker to mark authorization to enter. Despite the breeze, odors drifted from horse droppings from pony rides and caged farm animals that could be fed by grain sold by vendors. At the center of the area, hot dogs and cotton candy were sold.

Alex and Maddy headed to the merry-go-round as the first ride and sat on adjacent horses until deciding to switch to a carriage where they sat close together in the small seat. When the ride ended, they walked to arcade games, and Alex won a stuffed bear, handing it to Maddy. She offered to pay for dinner if he could outshoot her at a booth where tin ducks slid along a track with target circles on the facing side. Alex fired the laser weapon five times and struck two; Maddy knocked over three ducks with her shots. She raised her hands in victory, and he offered to increase the stakes. In the following contest, they scored in reverse: she with two, Alex scoring three times. Instead of a third round, they agreed to split the dinner bill. Their shooting success earned them another stuffed animal, and Alex handed the winning prize to a little girl walking by holding her mother's hand.

Clouds moved in and the temperature dropped. Maddy rubbed her upper arms.

As they were walking, Maddy said, "This event wasn't held when my kids were young; they would have loved it. I miss my children. Of course, they were a big part of my life, especially because Peter was gone so much. I got them ready in the morning, drove them to school and home, and was with them until they went to bed. I'm sure you miss your daughters."

"I do. While they're young, you get to share many things, visiting Santa in winter and trick or treating in fall. Christmas was the highlight. You grumble about the preparations but secretly enjoy it all. We could never buy an artificial tree, always a real one with the pine scent permeating the house. As they age, you find new activities to take them, expanding to trips on vacation. But eventually, friends and boyfriends replace you as their main interest. It's natural, and I wouldn't want them to cling, but there's a void."

"In a way, I'm fortunate in that I still have kids—my students. They're not *mine,* and as principal, I don't interact with them as their teachers do, but schools keep you in touch with youthful, energetic boys and girls on the cusp of adulthood."

"Now we can be the kids. Let's go on the Ferris wheel."

By mid-afternoon, they had been on every ride, played nearly every game, and purchased cotton candy, the sugar coating their mouths. As they sat on a bench, Alex asked, "What's the big surprise for tonight?"

"We're going dancing," Maddy said, her voice elevated. "You used to love to dance."

Alex pulled his head back and looked at her. "I haven't been dancing since, well, since you, or at weddings."

"You'll be fine. Drive me back to my house, and I can make something simple for our dinner, probably salmon, and we'll go to the dance in a converted barn. Park your car on the street, and we'll take mine."

On the way back to the motel, he thought about the plan, drawing out memories of dancing with Maddy. She was far better, but most of their movements were slow as they favored the softer melodies and clung together until the recording stopped. Afterward, they raced to one or the other's off-campus apartment.

~ * ~

Returning to her house that evening, he knocked on her door and was taken aback by her dress, which ended slightly above her knees; her face was carefully made up, with her eyes as the main focus. The lashes and liner brought out the color of her striking pupils. Before going inside, he stared at her for seconds. Glasses of white wine were on the dining room table; she handed him one and left to finish the meal preparation.

"Can I help?" he asked.

"No, it's an easy meal; it won't take me long."

Alex went into the living room and paced until she called to him. They sat across from each other, using the night's planned activity to recall dancing while in college. Maddy reminded him that the first time they'd gone to a party with music and room to move around a bare floor, he'd been awkward but had soon loosened up and proved adept in time. They'd practice in her apartment when her roommates weren't around.

After the meal, he helped her take the dishes and utensils to the kitchen to be left in the sink until the morning.

They stopped at a light on the way, and Maddy turned to him. "I've never felt lonely while you've been here. It's going to be hard to see you leave."

Maddy pulled into the marked spaces near a large, weathered barn. The entrance was wide, and the music poured through the porous wood siding.

Once inside, they wasted no time finding a spot on the polished floor while the songs poured out of the scattered speakers. The first dance was fast; they circled each other, stepping lightly. Once over, the following song was a slow number. They joined outstretched hands, he put his arm on her back, and she touched his shoulder.

Later in the evening, they stood closer to each other, so there was no separation. Her hand had moved upward and pressed against the back of his neck. Alex's hand had rested on the upward curve of her buttocks. One time they held each other even as the music stopped.

"Let's go, Alex," she whispered.

"Back to your house?" he asked, breathing deeply.

"No, to your motel."

Pulling up to the motel, Maddy said, "Don't say anything, please."

In his room, he stood silently, and she drew close to him as if they were still dancing. Alex's arms were at his side when she approached, but quickly wrapped around her. They kissed, at first cautiously, soon without hesitation. He unzipped the back of her dress, and she stepped out of the garment and reached to undo his shirt.

Grabbing his hand, she led him to the bed and undid the buckle of his pants. Alex took off his loafers and pants, and for a moment, they both looked at each other in their underwear. Maddy sat on the bed, and with a gentle push, he leaned her back and lay on top of her, his hands taking Maddy's hair off her face. Alex could feel her breathing heavily. "I didn't—" Alex said before she put her hand over his mouth. She put her arms around him; they turned, and he reached for the clasp on her bra. Freeing her breasts, he stroked each, and she pulled at his briefs. His mouth probed hers, and they stripped fully without interrupting the kiss.

Before Alex could enter her, Maddy put her hands on his front shoulders. "We can't, Alex." Maddy dropped her arms to the side and lifted slightly from the bed. He extended his hand, and she grasped his fingers to pull herself up. Alex backed away.

"I'm sorry. I wanted—" Maddy said. She was covering herself as much as she could.

Alex looked at her. "We both wanted."

Maddy put on her underwear while Alex dressed. She picked up her dress and slipped her legs through it. Alex was behind her and zipped up the back.

"Thank you."

"I unzipped, so it was my job," he said with a half-smile.

Fully dressed, they sat on the bed, leaning against each other.

"We went too far and nearly did something that could have changed both our lives, especially mine, but yours, too. I don't trust myself enough now to be with you," Maddy said. "I thought I was simply lonely, missing intimacy, and reliving a memory. We were touching with our bodies when we were dancing, the temptation became overwhelming. But it's much more than any of that. Making love would have made it very difficult to see you leave and not to want more of what we nearly had. I hope you understand."

"I understand, and I don't know what we would have planned as the next step, but I couldn't have just returned home as if nothing had happened and forget. I wanted to continue here and after, whatever that meant. Seeing you naked beneath me is an image I couldn't have put out of my mind, especially when you were within distance. This whole time with you has been wonderful, but I should go home tomorrow."

"Alex, please stop by before you head home. I don't want this to be our goodbyes." She was crying.

~ * ~

At eleven the next morning, he pulled into her driveway and walked slowly toward the front door. She opened the door, took his hand, and led him to the couch. She sat on the other cushion.

"I didn't sleep at all, thinking about us when we college students. I loved you but maybe not enough when we were young. We should have talked more to make you understand my feelings. I did discuss my anxiety about the future after college, but didn't try hard enough; I didn't give you a chance. I never loved anyone else after you until Peter, and a part of me loves you now, but that can't be enough to betray my husband, seek a divorce, and risk losing the respect of my children, who love their father, even if he wasn't there enough.

"Last night I called Peter. The call woke him up in more than one way. We talked for a long time and agreed we would change our lives, be with each other more, and revitalize our marriage. He deserves that, and so do I. Our relationship was wonderful in college and in these last few days, too. I'll never forget you, never had. I'm sorry."

"Don't be. I didn't fight the decision in college. I was stunned, but had plenty of time to challenge you, and persuade you to reconsider, but didn't. I just licked my wounds and moved on. Perhaps I didn't love *you* enough to fight.

"Being with you now has resurrected feelings, surely, and if you'd said you wanted to start again with me last night, I don't know what I would have said or how I would have reacted. I don't want to be part of breaking up your marriage or impacting the relationship with your children. I wouldn't change anything about these last few days, and I will cherish them, but we both know this is the end of further contact."

They rose from the couch and kissed gently. Alex left, backing slowly out of the driveway and turning at the next corner so her house was no longer visible.

Six

After leaving, he drove without a destination, having no interest in returning home. In a town further south, he pulled into a gas station and called Bethany to tell her he would be traveling for a few days before returning.

"Are you all right? Did something happen?" She launched questions before he interrupted her.

"I'll explain when I get back, but no questions now. I just need time. Since I've been away, I've received calls on my cell phone about my previous company; I'm just not ready to return or deal with mundane issues."

"Where are you going?"

"I have no idea. Never far enough so the return-to-home trip is long, don't worry. Let your sister know I'll be back in a few days."

"Dad, please stop these pursuits. Each time you return home, you seem conflicted."

"I'll be fine. This is a pretty region; the leaves are turning, and I want to explore. I'll be back soon."

"I planned to drive to the house as soon as you returned." Bethany hesitated. "I was bringing someone with me, not Merideth. I'll bring him some other time."

"Him? Don't change your plans, and I would like to meet *him*. I'll be home by Saturday at the latest."

"Okay, but I can come the following weekend if you change your mind."

After she hung up, Bethany called her sister and explained her sense that their father was upset. "I told him I was going to bring Bradley with me to the house, but I wish I hadn't. However, he insisted. I want to be home alone to listen to Dad about the latest woman. I'm anxious to introduce my boyfriend and explain our shared plans for graduate school, but that can wait. I don't see how I can talk to Dad about the woman, Maddy, while Bradley's there. Could you come down next weekend so we can talk to Dad?"

"I can come; Taylor will understand. I thought our father would be more comfortable with you."

"You're wrong, Merry; he respects you as more adult."

~ * ~

Alex went through the rest of his messages. While most related to his former business, there was a call from Carolyn Lipinski. He called her back.

"Hi, it's good to hear from you," Carolyn said. "The older couple you helped are delighted. The damaged items were repaired or replaced, and the house looks wonderful. They wanted me to make sure you knew of their appreciation."

"It's good to hear your voice, Carolyn. I'm sorry I didn't get back to you sooner."

As if she could sense the reason for the delayed response, she said, "Alex, I wasn't calling to get details on your meeting with the other women. If there is a woman who was part of your past and can be part of your future, I would be happy for you, but I don't need to know what happened. That's not why I tried to reach you."

"I'm still sorting everything out, but I am certain I enjoyed the time I spent with you. Please tell that older couple I'm glad for them, but the credit belongs to you."

After hanging up, he thought about the recent time with Carolyn and how much he liked being with her, but his mind was still spinning from what had happened with Maddy.

In going through the messages on his phone, he also saw that Jack Crabtree, the man who'd bought out his business, had called twice. The new owner was a broad-shouldered, affable individual who had played tackle on his college team. While competitors in business, Alex and Jack had a long friendship; he and Pietrina had often been to Jack's house for dinner and vice versa. Periodically, they shared industry gossip and information on new products and services.

"Is everything okay?" Alex asked.

"The business is doing great. My agents and those coming from your organization blend well and share leads. Two of your former reps left: one to retire and the other to go into an unrelated business. I hired two new, experienced agents and assigned them some of the accounts you handled.

"One of the new hires jumped right in, and the accounts seemed pleased; the other hire was a mistake. Three of your clients have threatened to go elsewhere. I can assign another agent to the customers, but I'm afraid they are so turned off, a new face won't help. I'm not worried about the revenue loss, but if word gets out to all your old accounts, we'll have a big problem. You'll recognize who the customers are.

"If you could call them, reassure the clients we will assign our best agents, and tell them you have confidence in my agency, I would be grateful. I can transfer this call to my secretary to give you their names and contact information."

Alex called the former clients and assured them of the new company's commitment. The calls reminded him he missed his former business and the people he dealt with.

~ * ~

Settling in after returning home on Friday, he went to town to collect his mail and buy food for the next few days. He thought about Bethany's *friend*; was he more than a friend; would there be an announcement? He reasoned Bethany would have told him about a serious relationship, or if Merry knew, she likely would have spilled the beans. Going up and down the grocery store aisles, he passed the items he needed, lost in thought about his daughter's arrival. Once he purchased and later put away the groceries on the kitchen shelves and the refrigerator, he sat in the living room and thought about Maddy.

~ * ~

He showered and dressed slowly in the morning, looking at the clock repeatedly. At one o'clock, the front door opened, and his younger daughter stood in the doorway with a tall, brown-haired man behind her. She grabbed the man's arm, pulled him in front of her, and introduced Bradley Rallings. The two shook hands, and Bethany stood between them to embrace her father.

"He has a monied name; that could be a good thing," he whispered in her ear.

Bethany led both to the living room. She explained she had met Bradley at college, and they were immediately a couple. She went on to list his good qualities. While she spoke, her boyfriend moved closer to her on the couch and squeezed her thigh when she complimented him.

"I'm glad to meet you, Bradley, but what's the announcement?"

"We have many of the same classes and want to go to graduate school—together," Bethany answered. Bradley smiled, displaying rows of perfectly aligned, polished teeth. His stare at his daughter convinced Alex the young man loved his child. It flashed in his mind that the couple was about his age when he was with Maddy.

"I sense you've selected a university."

"We have; it's Longridge University in lower Illinois."

"Do I have to pay Bradley's tuition as well as yours?" Alex joked.

"No, Dad, and not mine either. We want to get jobs on campus or locally and be independent. Besides, you're unemployed," she joked.

They discussed their plans and Bradley's background for the rest of the day, avoiding discussing Alex's time with Maddy. Having said few words when they first came in, the boyfriend grew more comfortable and participated animatedly in the conversation. By the time the young couple was ready to leave, Alex had liked Bradley, was impressed with how attentive he was to his daughter, and that they were in love. With the recent time spent with Maddy, he realized Bradley was more mature than he had been at a similar age. In the morning, Bethany was departing, she came down early, and Alex said how pleased he was to see her in a relationship with such a caring man.

"Don't you ever call him Brad?" he asked.

"No, Dad, and our friends don't shorten their names. We know guys named Michael and Peter, but you can never call them Mike and Pete. If you add a y at the end, they'll never talk to you."

"I guess I should have had him call me Alexander," he joked.

After the teasing, she hugged her father, her eyes brimming, and went upstairs to get ready to go. He didn't have to wait long before getting a call from his other daughter, who said she wanted to visit him on Friday. Alex asked if her husband would be coming too, and she explained he was going on a planned camping and fishing trip with his friends.

"Are you the other half of the tag team? I suspect you've been talking to your sister."

"We did talk," she answered non-committedly.

He couldn't recall the last time his older daughter had come alone to see him. While she didn't mention how long she'd be staying, he was hoping Merry wouldn't leave until Sunday. He thought of her probing about his time with Maddy. Bethany would not hesitate to ask him questions on personal topics, but Merideth lacked her sister's directness. He also hoped they could discuss the sense of estrangement he felt from her.

When she arrived late Friday, he was pleased to see her enter the house carrying a suitcase. They hugged, and Alex thought her hold lasted longer than usual. He led her into the living room, taking her case and putting it near the stairs leading up to the bedrooms.

"What's that delicious smell?" she asked.

"I'm cooking a loin of pork for dinner, which I hope is still one of your favorites."

"I thought we'd go out for dinner, but that's fine. I love pork and haven't had it for a long time."

"I want to spend as much time with you as I can without waiters interrupting and the noise of other conversations drowning out our talking. Take your suitcase to your room, and I'll make tea. I have your favorite brand."

She unpacked the few things she'd brought and went back down. Merry smiled as she looked at the cup he held while handing her another. The lettering was *Best Dad* on the ceramic.

"Okay, are you ready to be grilled?" she asked, while dunking the tea bag. "I may have to take notes because Bethany will want a detailed report. General question: how was your trip to see Maddy?"

"Fine; it was nice to see her again."

Merry laughed. "If you think you can get away with short responses, you are sadly mistaken."

Alex breathed in, but before he spoke, he looked at his daughter, and as often in the past, he was reminded of how much she looked like her mother. After she had grown into a woman, he'd call her Pietrina by mistake. "I'm still struggling over what happened." He went over the specifics cautiously, avoiding details that would dismay his daughter.

"What was it like to be with a woman you once loved before you met Mom?"

"I thought we'd talk mostly about history, but it got complicated as memories of old feelings were mentioned. Maddy is still the same person I was once drawn to."

"Didn't she end the relationship in college?"

"Yes, and we talked about that at length, and she explained I wasn't there for her when she needed me back then."

"And *that* was the only reason for the breakup?"

"Before I left, she said our feelings for each other likely did not sustain us beyond college. I agreed, but I don't think either truly believed it. I was too focused on milking the last days of college—the parties, the drinking—and wasn't attentive to what she was anxious about, especially how we would stay together after graduation."

"Did you spend a lot of time together on this trip?"

"Yes, nearly all the time I was there."

"I think you'd mentioned to Bethany or me she was married. Wasn't her husband concerned?"

"He was on a business trip."

"Dad, did something more happen you're not telling me?"

"Merry, you know I loved your mother deeply, and you probably thought she was the only woman I intensely cared about—"

"I'm a grown woman, and maybe I had that fantasy as a child, but not now."

"I'm being vague, but let me answer by saying we put ourselves in a situation that could have had a damaging outcome, but we both showed restraint at the right time. I left soon after. The past and the present blended, and feelings for her overlapped. If I had avoided wanting to know why she left me, we could have had a pleasant conversation about our college years.

"Still, getting into a discussion about our prior relationship led to deeper discussions beyond our former involvement. Once my emotions were no longer distorted by residual anger, I saw the reasons I loved her. When I was with her, we were as comfortable with each other as we once were, but the circumstances were different."

"Meaning she's married, and if I were to guess, unhappily so," Merry said.

"She also has children and a career."

Alex was seated on the couch, and Merry was in a facing chair, but she got up, sat beside him, and hugged him. Tears settled on her lower lashes. "I'm sorry, Dad. You were hurt once again."

"This has been difficult, and we can talk more, but dinner should be nearly ready. Why don't you join me in the kitchen, and we can get the meal ready?"

At dinner, Alex talked about his meeting with Bradley. "He seems like a nice guy."

"He is," Merideth said, "and he cares about Bethany. They've been together for almost six months, and it's serious. I know she loves him."

"Why didn't your sister tell me about him sooner?"

"Dad, a lot has been going on in this family for the last few months; she didn't think it was time until now."

They talked more about Maddy and later watched television for a few hours. Alex went upstairs while Merry stayed on the couch, stretched out with a blanket over her legs.

While undressing, Alex listened for the sounds from downstairs: the television was off, and he heard her talking, likely briefing her sister, he supposed. He'd missed the noise and often slept poorly in the quiet absence of his children. The memories of his married years haunted him, and the images of his former wife came vividly to mind. But hearing his daughter downstairs, he fell asleep quickly.

At two o'clock, he woke and heard the television was back on. Unlike her sister, Merry was always late to bed and awakened later in the morning. He put on his robe over his pajamas and went downstairs. Merideth was sitting up, the blanket over her feet. The tv volume was low, and she wasn't looking at the screen. Alex went downstairs, lifted the blanket, tossed it on a chair, and sat next to his daughter. Looking toward her, he saw tears running down her cheeks.

"What's upsetting you, Merry?"

"Mom never called me Merry; it was always Meridith, never the diminutive. Sometimes you think of the little things which bring up everything, especially while in this house."

"You miss her terribly, I know." He put his arms around his child and held her while she cried. Later that night, Alex went partially down the stairs, looked into the living room, and saw Merry had gone to bed, leaving the blanket on the couch.

They talked more about his trip to see Maddy and Bethany's boyfriend at breakfast.

"Do you think she'll marry Bradley?" Alex asked.

"Yes, my sister is so innocently open, sharing specifics I'd never mention about a relationship, but illustrates how much she loves him and her excitement about the future. If they do wed, Bradley will be a good husband for her."

"What do you want to do today?" he asked.

"I keep in touch with my friend Joanne, you remember her, I'm sure. She still lives in town and wants to meet with me. She's getting married and wants to tell me about it; she may want me to be a bridesmaid. Hopefully, you don't mind. I'll still have plenty of time to spend with you until I leave Sunday morning."

"That's fine, honey. I'll take you to dinner tonight."

Alex was raking leaves in the front yard when she returned in the afternoon. Merry changed to jeans and a sweatshirt and found the other rake. For a few hours, they piled leaves and collected them into bags. They drove into town and ate at a steakhouse.

In the morning, he rose early, regretting his daughter leaving. An hour later, Merry came downstairs and looked at her father.

Alex said softly. "I will miss you."

"You're going to make me cry again, and I've had enough of that already."

He pointed toward the table in the kitchen, and she sat facing him. While they drank coffee and nibbled on rolls, Alex said, "This house reminds you so much of your mom that coming here is hard. Is that why I haven't seen you much since your mother and I separated?"

"I was so confused, believing you two had everything. I couldn't accept that the decision was mutual, as you and Mom had described. The fault had to be uneven; someone had to blink first, likely you, I thought."

Merry paused and drew in a deep breath. "I was angry with you because I was convinced you would have seen signs of her illness better than Brian, and you would have encouraged her to get help earlier. You know Mom avoided doctors, but you could have pushed her. Brian did his best with Mom, but he never knew her the way you did and could get her to overcome her stubbornness as you could. I believed that for a long time; I clung to Mom and backed away from you. I became close to her new husband but *never* saw him as a father, just as a good man who made my mother happy."

"I could sense you were backing away. At times, it was obvious and other times subtle."

"But you had Bethany, and maybe I was jealous of that. I know you and Mom didn't show favoritism when we were growing up, but Bethany and I picked sides, even if you didn't. That was immature, I know."

"You know I love you equally, as did your mother, don't you?"

Merry laughed. "My sister and I were convinced once that loving us was a requirement of parenting, and if you didn't, the least favored or the most troublesome would be taken from you. Of course, that would have been Bethany."

"Do you keep in touch with Brian?"

She paused before answering. "No. I thought we'd grown close, and the closeness would continue after Mom died, but a week ago, he called me after I repeatedly tried to contact him by phone and text. He admitted he's been avoiding me, explaining that I reminded him too much of my mother, and it was hard to move on."

"You do look like Pietrina, more so than Bethany."

"I should get ready to leave. My fisherman-husband will be home late in the afternoon, hopefully bringing some caught fish. To be honest, I wanted to see you and encouraged him to go with his buddies."

"How are things with him?"

"You know he's a good guy, but we started having discussions about children, or at least I have. I want to start a family while I'm young. He feels we should wait, need both incomes, he's not ready—all sorts of reasons. Our last conversation—rather an argument—occurred before arranging his trip with the guys."

"I hope you have children, but of course, only you two can determine the timing, although I bet Bethany had some thoughts."

"Bethany has opinions on everything and is anxious to be an aunt. But who knows, she may be a mother before being an aunt."

Alex lowered his eyebrows and looked at his daughter before grinning. "Whichever happens first, I'll still be a grandfather."

Merry got up from the table and went upstairs. Alex stayed seated, dreading the returning quiet after she was gone, but he was comforted by the renewed closeness and the ease in talking about feelings. He carried her suitcase to her car and waited outside. The wind had picked up overnight, and the forecast was cloudy with the threat of cold rain.

Before Merry got behind the wheel, she asked, "Are you going to locate the third woman? Wasn't her name...Maria?"

"Bethany said she was easy to find, but I have no interest now. I need time."

"I'll share our discussion with my sister and tell her not to bug you for more details. But you know her, so don't be surprised when you soon get a phone call. She loves you, as I do, and is concerned."

They hugged, neither willing to step out of the embrace until a passing car horn sounded and distracted them. Alex stayed outside long after she was gone.

~ * ~

As his elder daughter had predicted, Bethany called him a few days after Merideth left, offering to visit. Alex made it clear he would not add more to the conversation he had with Merry, which he was certain the two had discussed. Bethany tried to interject questions, but he rebuffed her inquiry. Alex guessed her interest in visiting was lessened by his refusal. She changed the subject and asked about his reaction to her boyfriend. Alex was complimentary, and the issue of a visit didn't come up again.

"Don't forget, Dad, I have the information on your third ex-girlfriend, so call me when you want to know."

"I'm not ready, not yet anyway."

Over the next few weeks, Alex had been questioning whether he wanted to stop. The time with Maddy had been so debilitating he wasn't sure he could go through a visit to a third, former relationship. Maria Ribiero had a common first name, but she was hardly ordinary.

For a month, he thought about his next step. He called Carolyn and apologized to her for being abrupt in their last phone call, but she assured him she took no offense and appreciated his call. He told her he missed her, as if the words had formed without thought.

His next call was to Bethany, and after the greeting, he said, "I'm ready now."

She knew what he meant and offered to come home that weekend.

"I'll be glad to see you. Since returning from my trip to see Maddy, I've thought about this whole effort and decided to finish it. Bethany, I'm glad you brought Bradley with you last time, but could you come alone for the weekend? I'd just like to spend time with you."

Bethany arrived so early on Saturday that Alex was still out shopping. Pulling into the driveway behind a car he didn't recognize, he went inside carrying two paper bags. His daughter met him at the door, taking one of the packages from him.

"Whose car is that; it's not yours?"

"It's Bradley's—we swapped cars this weekend, and he'll change the oil and check the engine on my car. He's pretty mechanical for an intellectual."

"He's that smart, huh," he said, knowing her likely response.

"Yes, he picked me."

After emptying the groceries, they ate an early lunch and talked.

"You're not going to tell me more about Maddy than what Merry shared, are you?"

"Honey, I need to put the time with her aside and not carry those memories to a visit with someone else from my past. As I've said before, I'm not looking to make comparisons or go spouse shopping. I'm glad to see that Carolyn and Maddy are healthy, have successful careers, and are delightful women, but I need to move forward."

"After you meet Maria, what next? Have you thought beyond this next meeting?"

Alex answered, "Yes, I have. I realize I've given up my occupation, my older daughter is married and may have a family someday, my younger is moving on, this house is too large for one person, and your mother is gone. I need to get a life, hopefully with a woman I deeply care for."

"You *have been* thinking," her voice faltered. Recovering, she said, "Let's get down to business. I found Maria Ribeiro. She kept her name, so it was relatively easy. I found out she is not married, at least not now. You mentioned she was artistic and had worked at an art museum when you knew her. I found her with that little information and assumed her approximate age. She runs a private gallery called *Pacific Views* and is an artist herself, an accomplished painter known best on the West Coast. You can check her history. Currently, she's living in Monterey, California, which means she's on the other end of the country. Social media contains many photos of her artwork but few current images. As an artist, I suspect she will be unlike the women you've reconnected with so far."

Alex nodded, "She was different before, so alive and energetic you thought you'd get an electric shock by touching her. As I did with the others, I'll call her first to see if she's interested before arranging a flight."

That afternoon, Bethany helped her father clean the house and store items in the basement. For dinner, they went out, talking across the table about relatives but mostly about Merry. Bethany told her father the issue of children had been driving a wedge between Merry and her husband. After dinner, they went to the movies, and upon returning home, Bethany said she was tired and went to bed. Midmorning, she left. As he walked back into the house, he said aloud, "The adventure continues."

Part 3

Seven

Alex got the phone number for the Monterey gallery and asked to speak to Maria. The woman answering told him Maria was not available and politely refused to provide his former lover's cell or home number. He left his cell phone number with the comment they had known each other well, "a long time ago." That would be the first test, he realized; if she had no interest in talking to him or didn't remember him and their relationship, he wouldn't pursue it further. He didn't hear from Maria but dismissed the lack of response because of the time difference, given he'd left the message late afternoon, West Coast time. When three days passed, he felt the answer was clear. Early morning on the fourth day, the phone rang, and he picked it up without expectation.

"Is this you, Alex, my boyfriend of ancient times?"

"Hello, Maria; it's so good to hear from you." He paused and added, "Isn't it about six-thirty in the morning your time?"

"Yes, I'm an early riser and was eager to talk to you. I've known others named Alex, but when your message said you were someone I knew from long ago, I had to call you soonest.

I was out of town at a showing, but we can discuss what I'm doing later. First, I want to hear about you. The beginning question is: why did you contact me after all these years? I know I'm easy enough to find with the unchanged last name, but why the interest?"

Alex explained what he was doing, and he summarized his life, former wife, and her death. He also talked about his daughters and his retirement from his business.

When Maria said nothing after he'd finished talking, he wondered if she was listening, but her words showed she had been. What words?

"Alex, you've had a full life, and I'm sorry to hear about your ex-wife. I'm not great at reading people by their tone and intonations, especially over the phone, but I suspect you had a good relationship after the divorce and are proud of your daughters. I'm still puzzled at what you're doing—your adventure, as you called it."

Alex explained he was curious about the lives of three women who had meant a lot to him earlier in his life.

"Okay, let me see if I have this correct: there were three women—and I'm surprised it's only three—and I'm third on your list, or to put it upsettingly, I'm last on your list." She laughed to convey the humor in her statement.

"It's purely chronological, and if I reversed the order, you'd be first," he said, repeating the light tone of her remark. "And please don't refer to *The Batchelor* tv show. I've heard that often."

Maria laughed. "You must admit it's a good parallel."

They talked further, and eventually, she asked, "Now that we've been in touch, what's next?"

Alex said he would like to see her, fly to California if she agreed, and catch up further, but face to face.

For a few seconds, she didn't answer. "Alex, I was young, likely pretty back then, but those flattering words wouldn't apply to me now. I'm sure you've seen my Facebook and Instagram images, but they are old photos. Only the displays of my artwork are recent. I'm neither obese nor hampered physically, but just not the same as the perky girl you knew, and I'd like to believe, once loved."

"You're correct in describing my feelings about you when we were together, but wrong that I would have less interest in wanting to see you now. We all change with age; I'm not the same either. Back to my original question: would you mind if I flew out there to meet with you? If you are uncomfortable for any reason, we can stay in touch in this manner, and I would be understanding, but disappointed."

"I would love to see you, Alex, and I admit I've sometimes wondered about you and your life after our relationship ended, so please come."

The rest of the discussion was about logistics: the flights to Monterey, the timing, and where he could stay. At the end of their conversation, Alex said, "I'm looking forward to seeing you even more."

She echoed his words.

After hanging up, Alex checked into flights, called both daughters—recognizing the loving but competitive relationship—and explained his plans, adding a summary of his call to Maria. Both daughters offered encouragement, although he suspected a note of caution in Bethany's well-wishes. As with the other women he'd met with, he told Bethany and Merry he would stay for three days, although packing for five. He would call them if he stayed longer.

Before the flight, Alex thought about the past with Maria. The images of their early lives together played in his mind like the scripted scenes of a movie. He had graduated and got a job with an insurance firm, mainly selling to small businesses. After a year, he'd successfully established new clients and supported existing customers. A year later, the company had been looking to hire new staff. Before hiring, Alex's boss had suggested the two prime candidates under consideration spend a day with a current sales rep to see what the job entailed.

Maria Ribeiro had been the applicant assigned to shadow Alex. When they first met, Alex had stumbled over his words of introduction and explanation. He'd been struck by her attractiveness and dark complexion acquired from her Brazilian roots. Her petite nose would flare slightly in expression, her nostrils lifted by laughter or crinkling with displeasure.

Maria's flawless skin required little makeup to highlight her beauty except for added lashes circling her deep brown eyes. He recalled her expressive hands moving while she spoke, reminding him of an orchestra conductor in performance. Maria's smile came quickly and often, and she would touch to emphasize a point or ensure attention. Alex had suspected she'd been an athlete in college, apparent by her body—an assumption proved valid when they'd talked about her background while traveling to the customer meetings. They'd arranged the client visits for the day, starting at the office. Alex had offered to pick her up and got her address. When he'd arrived at her neat, well-tended house in a part of town unfamiliar to him, Alex had pressed the bell, and seemingly before the chime stopped, she'd flung open the door, clutched his arm, and turned him toward the curb where he'd parked the car.

"Whew," he'd said, "are you that anxious to start?"

Maria had stopped, and her face reddened. "Sorry; I live with my family, and they, especially my mother, are old-fashioned, checking out any male my age I know as a potential mate. It's embarrassing, especially with someone I just met, like you. My mom can be subtle and ask questions in a way you'd never know you're being sized up."

Alex laughed. "Is that typical of Hispanic parents?"

"We're Brazilian Portuguese. I don't know if it's true of all Latins."

Alex had noted he could detect a slight accent in her use of the word Portuguese.

Maria wore a skirt that stopped above her knees and was tight enough to illustrate she had a shapely body. Visiting a client who expressed an interest in risk insurance, Alex had felt he didn't have the potential customer's attention; the man's eyes often drifted toward Maria. At one point, the man had asked her what she thought about the company's product, and she'd answered adeptly, praising the organization without commenting on the unfamiliar services and offerings. The man's smile had reflected interest, although Alex wasn't sure in what.

On the way back to the car, she'd grabbed his arm to stop his walking. "I'm sorry. I was more a distraction than a help. I should have dressed more conservatively. I don't think of myself as that attractive, but it doesn't take much with some men."

Alex had laughed. "We're in luck; the next appointment is with a woman."

For lunch, they'd stopped at a small restaurant Alex called 'unique,' unable to come up with a better descriptor. Seated at the table, Alex had asked her what she thought about the morning.

She'd hesitated for a moment. "Alex, I hope I can trust you, but this is not what I want to do."

"I understand, but what do you want to do for a living?"

"I was an art major in college and would like to do something in the arts; I'm not sure what."

"Why did you apply for the job?"

"The money to have my own place, leave the hovering parents, and have boyfriends my mother won't scare off with talk of wanting grandchildren. I could do this job, but after this morning, it doesn't suit me. You are good at the job and enjoy your work, but it's not doesn't what I want to do with my life."

Alex had said, "Do you want to end the meetings now? I can tell my boss you decided not to accept the job, although he might think I scared you off."

Maria smiled, and Alex had realized he would miss her.

"I'll call him and tell him my decision, but let's go ahead with the appointments. Maybe what I learn from you about selling will be helpful in whatever career path I choose."

By four o'clock, they'd met with two additional customers, one potential and the other an existing client. Alex had asked her to handle the current policyholder, and he'd complimented her when she finished.

Dropping her off at her house, they had been awkward with each other saying goodbye. As she'd turned to go inside, he'd stopped her with his words.

"Since we won't be working with each other, I don't see a conflict if we went out, if you are interested."

She'd walked back to him, showed the dazzling smile she'd displayed throughout the day, kissed him on the cheek, and said, "Yes." Soon after, their being together went from platonic to intimate.

He yanked those memories from his mind, but went no further. He wanted to reminisce with her, hopefully filling in gaps, correcting his recollections, and describing how they had felt about each other back then.

~ * ~

Alex woke early on the morning of his departure and wondered what Maria looked like after hearing her warning about changes. She'd never boasted of her appearance and surprisingly understated her looks when they were young, even though many people remarked on her attractiveness.

Maria had been focused on fitness and would likely be fit and less altered by age than he was. Her self-description wasn't a deterrent but only a curiosity, but he remembered this whole search was a matter of curiosity.

The time with Maria would determine whether the trip and meeting were the right decisions or would bring out painful memories. However, even before he called her, Alex knew he had regretted the end of their relationship, but there had been no disagreement or resentment.

A cab pulled up in front of his house, and Alex loaded his suitcase into the trunk. He called his daughters and phoned Maria at the airport to say the flight was scheduled to take off on time, leaving a message on Maria's cell phone. The weather was ideal for flying; the clouds had abandoned the sky, and the cold, soft wind did little to impede the plane's forward motion. Alex had purchased a non-stop flight to San Francisco and a short flight to Monterey. He rented a car near the airport. The plane arrived early, and he drove around the area. A weak fog had collected at lower segments of the undulating streets and roads of Monterey and nearby Pacific Grove.

Driving to the motel, he pulled into the parking area and checked in. He called Maria, told her he was in town, and reconfirmed their plans for the following day. She responded she had to go to her gallery in the morning and added, "You can come with me; I'd like you to see it."

Anxious to meet with Maria, Alex left the following morning ahead of the arranged time in case he encountered traffic or made wrong turns on the way.

When he rang the bell, Maria opened the door dressed in shorts and a t-shirt; she was barefoot. Maria was sweating; droplets beaded on her bare legs and exposed arms, and a circle of sweat formed under her arms. Her dark brown hair was short with streaks of gray and was slicked back and moist, her face was lined at the corners of her eyes, and her lips were dry and bare of lipstick. Her skin coloring was lighter than he recalled. He remembered her pretty green eyes, which often signaled her emotions, and her small ears—he recalled teasingly questioning if she could hear well. A pair of wire-rimmed glasses were on the coffee table with large frames. But he also noticed the differences in her features from what he remembered.

As he looked at her face, the word that came to mind was *gaunt*— thinness not from exercise or diet, nor from age, but from illness. Wrinkles sliced across her forehead. Without makeup, the circles under her eyes were dark. Alex determined he wouldn't speculate, recognizing he'd arrived before she'd had time to prepare.

"You're early," she said, her voice lifting. "I'd hug you, but, as you can see, I'm damp and, take my word for it, somewhat rank. Come on in; I'll quickly shower shortly." Her tone toward Alex conveyed a lack of concern about his coming before arranged.

"I'm sorry; I am early. You ran track in college, didn't you? You kept up with the running." Looking down at her feet, he added, "I remember whenever you came indoors, you took off your shoes."

She laughed. "Still true. I walk around the gallery barefoot, but you can do so without seeming odd to artistic people. Don't apologize about being here early, but this is not the best image of someone you haven't seen for a long time." She sat across from him on a pink, cushioned chair. Despite her words, he thought she wasn't in a hurry to clean up.

They chatted for a few minutes; he complimented her on the house and the neighborhood until she excused herself to get ready. As she walked away, she said over her shoulder, "Help yourself if you're thirsty; the kitchen is over there." She pointed with her right hand without turning around. "It's too soon in the day for wine, but there are soft drinks."

He admiringly watched her firm buttocks and legs as she walked into the hallway. When she came back in half an hour, she was wearing an auburn sweater and gray pants; her face was made up, and she resembled the woman he recalled. Her cheeks had been full and rounded in his memory, reflecting her enjoyment of sugary foods and fast-food meals despite her physical process and activity. Her cheeks now seemed drawn in, as in frozen in a pucker. But to Alex, she was attractive and compelling, much like the woman he knew in their younger years. He laughed because she still wasn't wearing shoes, as if footwear were the last dressing item. He seemed drawn to women who hated shoes.

On the drive, their conversation was light: about his trip and briefly about her gallery. They drove south of the beach to Delmonte Street, past the Naval Post Graduate school and the marina pinned between two piers, and turned south on Washington Street.

The art gallery was a two-level brick building with a large window facing the street. A colorful canvas filled the window, and an awning shaded the front door. The glass door entrance was marked with stenciling of the gallery's name, Maria's signature in bold lettering, and the address of the building in smaller font.

The white and beige walls held paintings in an order Alex suspected had a purpose to the arrangement. He was struck by the vivid portraits, colorful beach images, and fall landscapes of multi-hues. Standing in the center of the room, Alex and Maria were approached by a petite young woman Alex estimated to be a college student and younger than Bethany. Maria introduced Rebecca and told Alex she would be his guide through the displays.

"I have to call a gallery owner in San Francisco about an art showing in the city to highlight artists from the towns and locations between Frisco and Los Angeles, appropriately entitled, *Between the Cities*. I've had a lot of luck in the region, with sales in Monterey and the surrounding area, but less so in the big city and places like San Jose, all north of here. There will be art critics there and hopefully a lot of buyers. Praises and purchases from the right people could boost my reputation further across the state. I shouldn't be more than an hour.

Becky will do a great job explaining everything; she's attending Monterey Peninsula College and works part-time to keep things in order here. She's also a fine artist."

Leaving the two standing there, Maria went toward the rear of the floor. Becky looked at Alex and said, "We can start the tour over there," pointing to a section on the right. The space was constructed specifically as an art gallery with high interior walls ideal for hangings. The blocked window kept light from brightening the room, and an overheard spotlight illuminated pictures in the darker section. The first area they toured contained a collection of landscape images; another area housed paintings of desert-like, arid plants and scattered trees, including cacti. Circling the room, they entered a portion of the gallery with more abstract images.

"Each section represents a different period in Maria's history, influenced by location and style she's admired in other artists. She didn't paint all these pieces and added the works of other artists from the area. I wanted to mix the styles, telling her the division might reflect an artistic fickleness, but I didn't win, as you can see. I even recommended she mark the painting by years, but I was shot down." Alex saw she was smiling, which meant she was not offended by being overruled. "Maria works hard and has been generating pieces continually for years, except in the period when—" Becky's face turned red.

"Except when?"

"Oh, you know; creative persons, writers, painters, all go through a period of what authors call 'writer's block,' when ideas disappear for a while."

"Becky, has anyone told you that lying and evasion are not your strengths, but I won't put you on the spot? I'll ask Maria."

"Thank you."

Maria took longer than expected, and an hour and a half later, she emerged from her office. She apologized for the delay. Becky used her boss's arrival to excuse herself, extended her hand to Alex, and left.

"I hope my assistant gave you a wonderful tour."

"She did a fine job; what's next?"

"Monterey has so many unique places to visit. I thought we'd go to Cannery Row, made famous by John Steinbeck. It's become touristy over the years, but still worthwhile. I think you once mentioned reading his books when we were together."

"Yes, you're right—I'm impressed by your memory."

"I remember a lot about you, probably things you'd wish I'd forgotten," she said with a laugh. "There are some nice places where we can have a light lunch. I'll take you to Carmel for dinner, my treat."

They went to Cannery Row and toured the area, viewing sites emphasizing the early fish processing industry; paper signs offered tours, and copies of the Steinbeck novel were in every bookstore window. At about one o'clock, they stopped at a small restaurant Maria declared was the best place locally for fish and chips. While enjoying the meal, which Alex said was delicious, he used the time to discover details of her life.

"We were together for less than two years; you worked for a local museum, but soon after, you went west. We were both sad and tried to keep our relationship going, but the distance was too great."

"Yes," Maria said, "We tried for a while, and although we stayed in touch, it wasn't working. That first job was like being the assistant to the assistant, learning nothing except the coffee preferences of the staff. I stayed in the job and liked the people, but wasn't developing any useful skills. In Denver, where I went next, I was a true assistant in an art gallery, taking on responsibilities and learning the business side of art. I used the experience to get another job managing an art gallery.

"Both jobs helped me to do what I'm doing now. I was taking art classes and developing my skill and style simultaneously. Later, I moved to Monterey with a boyfriend, but he left, and I stayed. My paintings were gaining attention mostly as a regional artist, and eventually, I purchased the building. The gallery has two floors; the upper level was a storage area before I bought it, and I changed the second-floor space, setting it up as a studio. You wouldn't want to go up there; it's a mess."

"How would you define your style of painting?"

"I'm not sure if you mean the type of instruments and paints I use or the school of painting or influence on my method. I view my way of creating as eclectic. I paint with oils, and, admiring Andrew Wyeth, I often use the dry-brush method, as he did. The location influences my style. As you may have noticed, I painted some in a desert-like region. Before taking the gallery job in California, I took a year off and spent the time in New Mexico and Arizona creating the pictures of deserts you saw."

"How long did the relationship last to cause you to move here?"

"Almost six years. I tend toward long-term involvements." As soon as she finished, Maria's face reddened. "You and I had something special, and it was so early in our—"

"Maria, I understand. Besides being young, we had to build our careers, and looking where we both are now, we made the right choices, even if it hurt."

"When I got the job in Denver, I spent all my time learning, but sometimes in the early years, at night, I cried, thinking about you. It's so odd to be here together now, after so many years."

"It took me a while to get over losing you, but there was no animosity, fault-finding, or hidden reasons. Perhaps I thought the separation was temporary, or I could move to where you were. But after you were gone, I wondered why you couldn't have tried harder to find the kind of job you wanted closer to where we lived.

"I met with another woman from my past, and she said our involvement—hers and mine—ended because we didn't love each other enough to overcome the problem separating us. I probably thought the same about you and me when you left. When you're that young, thoughts are self-centered, as mine were."

"Alex, we decide at various times in our lives and different expectations in a serious relationship. You can't judge your feelings for someone so far in the past from your current perspective. In our situation, we were serious, but not necessarily compatible. We both had forming careers but no other challenge testing our relationship. Look at our lives now: you have two daughters, and I have none—by choice. I live in a warm climate; you live with long winters." She shivered at the thought. "I could list other examples, but we did not continue because we matured into different people. I don't recall we ever said we loved each other; we might have, but saying those words was loaded with commitment and obligation, and neither of us wanted it then."

"You evolved from an impetuous woman into a wise, reasoning person, making your point in part. We do change."

"I don't know what you expect to come from your trip here or what can happen, but I'm anxious to find out," Maria said.

Alex looked at her for a moment and, as if breaking from a trance, said, "I'm looking forward to spending time with you. So, what's the next tourist stop?"

"There are so many beautiful and wonderful places to see and visit: Seventeen Mile Drive, Carmel, and Highway One, which climbs upward bordering the ocean."

They headed to the entrance to 17 Mile Drive. Before they arrived, she highlighted the major attraction of the winding road to Alex and promised she would point them out as they traveled along the circular road. She explained that the concrete path wound around major golf courses, including Pebble Beach and Spyglass, where tournaments were held. The trail stayed flat at the ocean's edge, with views of waves smacking against the shoreline. A large rock near the land's end was colored white at one segment by bird droppings. Sea lions and pelicans occupied the rock. Seals clung to the rocky edge. They drove through a forested area, later parked at Spanish Beach, and walked down to the beach. Using a blanket Maria kept in her trunk, they sat on the dark sand.

While they watched the waves, Maria said, "Go ahead and ask the common question: why didn't I ever marry?"

"I wasn't going to ask, but I was thinking about it."

"I've come close, three times even." Her eyes closed partially, she added, "I had a dog I loved; he was more faithful and less fickle than any of the men I'd had a serious relationship with. I was involved with another artist, Rudy, short for Rodolpho, a photographer, for four years during the time he traveled extensively.

"At the end of that period in our relationship, he slowed his trips somewhat, and we spent much more time together over the next three years until we broke up. We never actually lived together, meaning we never co-owned a home. He had an apartment in San Francisco and a studio in Monterey where he worked on his photographs with a small storefront area to display and sell some of his works for extra money. Rudy never wanted to own a house with property; he traveled too often, and his assignments were rarely local.

"On the other hand, I wanted a house and everything with it. We varied our time together; I often stayed at his place in the city, and he came here frequently. We were comfortable, had no plans to marry, didn't see the need, and were both past the age of considering children.

"We never saw the oddity in the arrangement; even initially, we didn't miss each other with the same intensity new couples felt when they had to be separated, but we looked forward to being with each other when we could. But the weeks apart kept getting longer for him and me, although more often for Rudy, especially when he began traveling again. The enthusiasm faded. I cheated on him once, and I suspect he did as well, maybe more frequently. We called each other, but neither was the type to express feelings, so our conversations were primarily facts about what we were doing and the gossip about friends. I'm still amazed that artists so emotive in their art can find it difficult to express love in their communications.

"After winning a prestigious award for his works, Rudy was offered an excellent opportunity to take photos for a major magazine. The offer, based in Europe, was too tempting to pass up. His pictures were beautiful, capturing images better than I could with my brushes. I once asked Rudy what he loved photographing the best, and his answer surprised me; he said, 'Women kissing; it is the most beautiful and sensual image.' He wasn't heralding sexual orientation or any physical intimacy. He believed women kissed with artistry. Rudy said women can make kissing a form of lovemaking; for men, it's a prelude."

"Very perceptive."

"I suspect he was quoting his gay sister. I loved him and regretted not having said so." Pausing, she looked at Alex. "You're not saying anything."

"I'm not comparing what you had with him to our past relationship, but I don't know how anyone could leave you now, even for a career-enhancing assignment. However, as I've recently learned, involved people can still make choices detrimental to relationships."

"Sounds interesting; we'll have to talk more. While not unique with artists of all disciplines, there is the worry that our art can fall out of favor, and success shrinks or disappears, so I can understand his need to stay relevant and employed," Maria said.

"You mentioned there were three long-lasting relationships. Was Rudy the second, assuming the man you followed here was the first? Can you tell me about the third?"

She answered, "Rudy *was* the second. I don't want to discuss the last involvement. Even now, it's painful to mention and more than I want to share at this point—perhaps later. Friends have known about each relationship, but no one has been with me through all three. You are the only one I explained these relationships to. Isn't it coincidental that we both have had three great loves in our lives? Keep in mind that I've described long-term relationships; if I mentioned intense relationships, regardless of length, you'd be the fourth and the only other one. Your turn. What did your family think about the searches?"

"When I explained I wanted to find out about past loves, my daughters were skeptical. They think I'm regressing or going to the past because the future is uncertain."

"I once read the past is the only certainty in our lives."

"I'm continually amazed. How did you get so insightful?"

"It's not natural or inherited; I read a lot." She answered, smiling.

"Wait—what about death and taxes?"

"That's true about death, but many people find ways around taxes, especially around here. Okay, enough philosophy."

Alex talked about his time with Carolyn and Maddy and the different outcomes, not mentioning the incident in his hotel room with Maddy.

Maria looked at him. "How did you find numbers one and two?"

"Carolyn and Maddy," he corrected. "My younger found them. As you mentioned, you were the easiest to track down."

"I prefer numbers, except for me, of course. I never asked, how long are you staying?"

"I kept it open, figuring three days, and would see after that."

"I hope you'll stay longer to enjoy all the sights."

When they stood to go, Maria surprised him with a question. "Was your divorce truly mutual?"

"Pretty much," Alex answered, "but she concluded before I did. I told no one that. She remarried, so that may have been a sign."

They got back in the car and drove the rest of the way along the route. Maria slowed near a solitary tree on a stretch of land at the ocean's edge. "The Lone Cypress is a familiar landmark often photographed by tourists. I can identify with the tree at times in my life."

"But it seems deeply rooted," Alex said.

Maria laughed. "You are becoming metaphorical. Must be the air."

Maria drove to her house to change for dinner, and Alex got into his car to return to the motel. After changing, he headed back to her home. When she opened the door, he stepped back to see her fully; her skirt stopped above her knees, her black blouse was unbuttoned at the top, and she wore heels that lifted her and accented her calves.

"You look beautiful," he said.

"I hope I don't detect an inflection of surprise."

"No, appreciation."

For dinner, they drove to Carmel. Entering the picturesque city, she traveled past the main sections toward the beach, circling back to Mission Street, and pulling in front of the restaurant, a narrow building with red tablecloths on wood tables. Paintings hung on the beige walls with the artists' names on small plaques in the frame. Waiters scurried across the spaces between tables; conic lights were suspended from the ceiling giving a dim glow to the room. As a result, some patrons took glasses from their pockets to read the menu.

They noted that soft music came out of strategically placed speakers, and pleasant odors poured out of the kitchen when the waitstaff retrieved the orders. Alex looked around and nodded, saying: "Nice; great atmosphere."

Maria explained. "Carmel has always had charm and a mixture of visitors and residents. In the late sixties and early seventies, hippies occupied the beach, but the houses are expensive now, as you imagine. The golf courses attract serious players who can afford membership and green fees. Tourists flock to the well-tended town. Celebrities come here for the Pebble Beach tournament to watch the pros and invited amateurs. Clint Eastwood was once the mayor. As you can feel, the weather here is great. We deal with fog, especially in the warmer months, but we are accustomed to driving through the mist. Why are you staring at me?"

"I'm just trying to envision you when we first met."

"I have something that can help. When you called and said you were coming to visit, I went through the photos I kept in boxes, took out the ones with us, and put the pictures in an album. After dinner, I thought we could go back to my house and look at them."

Their meal arrived quickly, and the waiter lowered the plates to the table, unrolled the napkins at the side of the plate, and handed them to Alex and Maria.

Between forkfuls, Maria talked about the start of their relationship. "I told you about my heritage when we first met. You researched Brazil and even learned keywords and phrases. You once came to my house for dinner and used Portuguese words. I was impressed, and so were my parents. I also admired your openness. The U.S. has matured, but a white-skinned man and a dark-color woman drew stares when we were together."

"You were feisty, you know," Alex said.

She laughed. "We had some good arguments. When we got loud, you told me to shut up in my language: *cale a boca*. You mispronounced it; I was doubled over, which ended the disagreement."

When they finished, the waiter returned to take their plates away and asked for their dessert order. Alex asked for a few minutes and, turning to Maria, said, "Can we skip the sweet stuff and go back to your place to look at the pictures?"

At her home, she told Alex to sit on the couch while she uncorked a bottle of wine and retrieved the album. The green cover was unmarked, but when she opened the first page, Alex saw an image of them staring at each other with total concentration and caring. The following snapshot was from a costume party with individuals all around them in masks and outfits. Alex was dressed as the Lone Ranger, and she was Tonto, with a buckskin skirt. He pointed at their images.

"You didn't want us to wear those outfits; you argued yours made you seem subservient. But you got a lot more notice than I did."

"It conveyed submissiveness and was sexist."

"At least I didn't ask you to say '*kemo sabe.*'"

Both laughed at the following picture. Alex wore a wide-brimmed leather hat, a fringed vest, and faded jeans. Maria was in jeans, a denim blouse, and sneakers.

"We looked like hippies; all we needed was a flowered Volkswagen van."

Alex added, "We both took off from work and went on the road, camping out or staying at a rented cabin."

They looked through the remaining photos, all with them together at various activities and times. Anyone else in the pictures was solely background, as if the camera could only focus on them. Some shots were blurry, likely because of a reluctant volunteer photographer who was eager to finish. The seasons were clear by the clothes they wore and the background.

One image was of Maria solely while they were at the beach, and as Alex recalled, he had been taking the picture. Maria was in a bikini, looking out toward the ocean. He'd taken a long time to press the button at the camera's top. He remembered staring at her until she'd turned toward him and smiled, providing the perfect moment to snap the shutter. When they reached the album's end, Alex turned the pages to the first photograph, the one in which they were simply looking at each other.

"Did we make the right decision? After we broke up, I wondered, and even seeing you now, I have the same thought," he said.

"I missed you; I told you that. But I would have been miserable had I not moved on and begun my career in the direction it needed. Talent in any artistic field needs exploration to determine if we could excel, an egotistical notion, as if people in other occupations couldn't feel the same draw.

"If we'd stayed together, my frustration and cowardice would have spilled into our relationship and poisoned it. These photographs remind me of how wonderful our time with each other was, and I have so many unspoiled memories. I had following relationships, most often with men in my field, less so in my later years, but those involvements were never an attempt to duplicate our relationship. I know this sounds cold and may not be fully accurate, but I had moved on, and obviously, the same was true for you."

Alex said, "Just the other day, I was thinking: why didn't I go to Denver to see where things would go? However, I was recently reminded by someone: you can't assess past choices by your current situation or mindset."

"A wise person, probably one of the women you recently encountered."

The album was still open on Maria's lap, and she grabbed the hardcovers and slammed the album closed. Alex looked at her, his forehead wrinkled, his head tilted, and his eyes narrowing.

"Alex, let's not talk about the past while you are here. Instead, we should focus on the right now. It's wonderful to have you here and not just to reminisce. As you've noticed so far, there is so much to see and do here."

"Fine, but I'm not here as a tourist, and you shouldn't feel obligated to entertain me or be my guide. I came here to see you."

Maria leaned over and kissed him, the duration of the connection interrupted when the thick album fell to the floor.

Before Alex left her house, she told him what to wear for the next day's activities without being specific about her plan. "Put on a short-sleeved shirt, sneakers, and pants of any sort."

Alex looked at her, the puzzlement showing on his face. "You're not going to tell me anything else, are you?"

"No," she said as she walked him to the entrance, drew closer, and kissed him lightly at the door. "I have to do things at the gallery, come to my house by around one. Get your rest; you'll need it."

The next afternoon, he showed up dressed as she instructed. Maria had also mentioned the front door would be open, and he could enter in case she was still getting ready. Immediately, he smelled the coffee perking on the stove and followed the aroma into the gray-walled kitchen with white appliances. A cup, sugar, and milk were beside the pot; she yelled she would be there in a few minutes.

When she came down in slow, exaggerated steps, Maria wore a cotton blouse and white shorts that left her long, tan legs in view. Her hair was combed back, still moist from a shower. She held a tennis racket in one hand, and in the other, she dragged another racket with a pair of white shorts wrapped around the handle. She gave him that racket and explained, "We're playing tennis like we used to, but I should warn you, I'm a lot better now, so be prepared for defeat."

"You were always cocky on the court, but remember who won most times, and I let you win on the rare occasions you were victorious. I didn't want you to be upset." He was grinning.

"Okay, big shot, let's wager. If you beat me, I'll buy you a fifty-dollar bottle of wine."

"Make it a hundred, and you're on."

"The shorts belonged to an ex-boyfriend and were washed and pressed. He was about your size, a little less paunchy," Maria said.

"Oh, the victory will be sweet," Alex said.

Maria pulled her car from the garage and drove the short distance to a club where she was a member. The court was fresh-scrubbed, and the taut net was attached to the silver poles. Positioning themselves on opposite sides, Maria offered to serve. Alex spread his legs and shook the racket to warm up. Her first stroke came toward him in a straight line, and he ducked. When he looked toward Maria, she was doubled over, laughing.

"I wasn't ready," Alex explained.

Her next stroke was a soft lob lifting high before crossing the net.

"Very funny," he said.

Alex held his racket tightly and waited for the next volley. As the ball headed to his side of the net, he pulled his arm back and struck with all his strength. The ball flew upward, lofting over the wire fence, and landing on the grass.

"I know just the variety of wine you can purchase," Maria teased.

They played competitively in a few exchanges, although Maria was outscoring Alex. After about a few hours, Maria lowered her racket and said, "Have you been trounced enough?"

Not answering her teasing question, he said, "I know it's too late for lunch and too early for dinner, but I'm hungry. Is there someplace near we can get something to eat?"

"In the clubhouse, they serve light stuff: sandwiches, bagels, et cetera."

They sat at a wood-topped counter; a woman approached them for their order and stared until Maria and Alex selected.

"She must be closing up," Maria said, looking around at the empty tables. "After we're done here, I'll drive you back to the motel to change; come to my place in an hour. I'll find something to nibble on."

They stopped at a wine shop containing rows of wine segmented by country of origin; California bottles were the largest section. They separated, each going down aisles. Maria stopped mid-aisle, waved a bottle of Malbec, and called to Alex, "This is the one."

On the way to her house, Alex wondered where this was going, considering the trip as the final leg of an effort to meet up with three women from his past. Compared to the time—measured in days—spent with Carolyn and Maddy, this was likely going to be the longest. He'd spoken to his daughters, being non-committal about his thoughts on Maria. Describing the area's beauty, he avoided considering emerging feelings toward her.

While equally involved in an active profession, as were the others, Maria seemed to have greater schedule flexibility and could easily allocate time with him. He viewed his days with Carolyn as pleasant, a blend of nostalgia and enjoyment when they reconnected; the time with Maddy was intense, conflicting, and emotional.

With Maria, the sightseeing, the banter, and ease were free of assessing shared emotional feelings. But something was brewing, different from the times with the others, unclear and undiscussed. He knew he needed time to explore; there was more to Maria as if she were holding back some element of her life still impacting her, but it was too soon to explain. Even in prolonged discussions about the years since their early relationship, he felt she skipped segments, like reading an engaging novel with a page missing in a chapter.

Returning to her house, he saw she was wearing sweatpants and a long, white t-shirt. Her face was lightly made up, and the forming rings under her eyes were visible beneath the makeup. They walked together into the living room and sat on the couch.

"I have some fruit slices, cheese, and crackers to munch on. I won't open the costly wine now; it's too good for such snacks. I have others."

She left the room and returned with a bottle of white wine and a food tray. Putting the items on the coffee table, she ran back to the kitchen to retrieve the glasses.

"In case you didn't catch the hint about the expensive wine, I'm hoping you still haven't set a time to leave, at least to lose again in tennis."

"I just don't want to get in the way of your work."

She reached over and kissed him. "Did I answer your question?"

"Yes, but you raised new ones."

Maria said, "I can be abstract in my art, but I'm a realist in life. I know you'll leave, just not soon." After pausing, neither spoke, she added, "Stay with me tonight. If I'm making you uncomfortable, I have a second bedroom."

Alex was holding his wine glass as she spoke. Putting it down, he leaned forward and kissed her. At first, their lips were lightly pressed together, but soon the kiss deepened, and the space between their bodies lessened. They remained seated on the cushions until Maria stood, grasped his hand, and pulled him toward the stairs. At the top of the landing, only a nightlight illuminated the second-floor hallway, and the darkness was even greater in her bedroom. He held her, using his hands to explore her body; only her breasts were unreachable as her chest was so tightly against his. His legs struck against the bed frame, and his hands were against her legs, touching over the cotton of her sweats when he felt the pants slipping down, and his touch was soon on bare flesh.

"Maria, I can't see you."

She stepped back and said, "That's part of the mystique."

Alex felt her tugging at his belt, and he stepped out of his shoes and pushed his pants down. Both dropped onto the bed, Maria pulling him on top of her. She used her hand to caress his face and lowered the other hand to pull off her underwear. Alex did the same until they were naked on the bedcover, except she was still wearing the t-shirt. He tugged at the edge of the garment to lift it over her head, but she twisted and was on top of him. He lost his grip on her sole covering. She rolled off, pulled him back over her, and reached down to touch him.

They remained in an embrace for a while, their mouths still joined, and only a second, unsuccessful effort to remove her t-shirt was out of sync with the natural surge of passion. Maria guided Alex into her, and they moved slowly until her back arched, and he pressed deeper inside.

They both lay flat, sweating, the moisture showing on their bodies, except on Maria's covered chest.

"I'm glad we made love," Maria said.

"I wasn't expecting that to happen, but I should have remembered; you surprised me a lot when we were going out."

"I always hated condoms?" Her remark and his laughter broke the mood.

"If we hadn't used them, there could have been another Alex somewhere," he said.

He expected her to continue the banter, but instead, she said, "Let's change the subject."

"Okay, that's fine."

Turning toward him, Maria kissed him. "I meant what I said earlier; I realize there's a limit on our time together, but regardless, please check out of the motel and stay here."

He nodded, realizing his head rubbing against the pillow showed his response.

"I'm chilly and am going to put on the pajamas I have hanging in the bathroom," Maria said. "Sorry, you'll have to stay naked for the night, but I could be too late in the night."

"Are you ever going to take off the t-shirt?" he asked while turning on the light.

She took off the shirt, tossed it in his direction, and entered the bathroom with her back to him. Alex pulled the covers down and slid beneath the blanket, waiting for her. She returned and pressed against him, her arm extending across his chest until she slept. During the night, she didn't stir or wake.

He looked toward the other side of the bed in the morning and saw she was gone. Approaching her in the kitchen, he could smell the soap on her skin and put his hands on her waist. He reached around to untie the knot in her bathrobe. She took hold of his hands and kissed his palms.

Alex stepped back, "Are you being modest?" the last word accented.

She laughed. "Of course not; I just don't want you to be making comparisons to ancient remembrances of my body. You'd seen me naked a lot. Sit, and I'll cook some eggs. We didn't have much to eat last night."

"Your fault," he said as he pulled the chair back.

"I don't recall hearing any protests."

"I wouldn't mind passing up on another meal for the same reason—"

"Sorry, Casanova, I have to go into the studio this morning, but I'll be back in the afternoon."

Maria emptied the eggs onto the plates and carried bread in the other hand. Partially through the meal, she asked, "What would you like to do today?"

His forehead wrinkled, Alex leaned back, "How about nothing; just spend time together, no plans?"

"Sounds domestic. When I get back, I'll go shopping, pick up food, and make dinner," she offered.

"Since I have time while you are at work, I'll shop for you. I know where the supermarket is."

"Great; the list is on the refrigerator, and I'll leave you my credit card." She stood and kissed him. "Leave your plate and cup in the sink."

After she left, Alex showered, drove to the motel to check out, headed to the supermarket, and read through the list she had left. Unfamiliar with the store's layout, he roamed around the aisles until the cart was half-filled. Next, he added chicken and pork at the meat section, but he picked up some beef before leaving the open-refrigerated section. He turned the meat several times and, perplexed, looked at a young, attractive woman standing next to him. Sensing his stare, she turned her head toward Alex, and he smiled.

"Can you tell me how long it takes to cook beef this size and at what temperature?"

The pretty woman pulled her head back and said abruptly. "No, I can't," and hurried away. An older woman heard the exchange and offered instructions on preparing the meat.

"I don't understand the young lady's reaction."

The woman said, "She thought you were hitting on her."

Putting stuff away in cabinets and the refrigerator, he heard the phone ring but ignored the call. The message was from Maria apologizing, saying she was delayed longer than expected. He called her back and said all was under control. At about five-thirty, she opened the front door.

"Honey, I'm home."

He came to the door and kissed her, "Wise guy."

Maria sniffed deeply, "What's cooking?"

"I bought a roast; it's cooking in the oven, but it still has a way to go."

She threw her arms around him. "Wonderful. It's a shame you can never live in this state. I suspect you are a meat-eating conservative. To be eligible for residency in California, you must be a liberal vegetarian."

"Yeah, yeah. I saw those hamburgers in the freezer. How can I report you to the authorities?"

She looked toward the table. "You didn't use my credit card, did you? It's in the exact spot I left it."

"I forgot," he answered, shrugging.

"I'm going to change into something more comfortable. Open the good bottle of wine."

"How do you know it's good, anyway?"

"Because you paid for it," she said, disappearing up the stairs. Returning down, she wore shorts and a t-shirt with an image of the California flag in front. Alex handed her a glass, and they talked about her day. When she finished, Alex mentioned his errands, especially about what had happened at the supermarket.

"I was just asking a young woman how to prepare the meat; she got huffy and stormed away."

"Was she pretty?"

"Yes, she was attractive, but what has that got to do with anything?"

"She probably thought you were hitting on her."

"I can come up with a better line than how do you cook meat."

Maria laughed. "How did you figure out the cooking instruction?"

"An older woman—"

"A grandmotherly type, someone your age?" Maria interjected.

They both laughed, and she hugged him.

At dinner, Alex explained his daughters called him to check up and added, "You'd like my kids, and they would like you."

Later, they snuggled on the couch and watched a movie until Maria said, "Let's go to bed." In her bedroom, they undressed, and while the room wasn't as dark as the previous night, they were still operating more by feel than sight. She unfastened her bra from underneath, but Maria never took off the T-shirt. They both said the love-making was great afterward, but Alex was bothered.

He was awakened by the shower running in the bathroom and joined her. She yelled, "Don't come in!" when he opened the bathroom. Alex went back to bed. When she came out, her hair was wet, and she was wrapped in a bathrobe. "I'm sorry, and I know it's quirky, but I don't like sharing a shower."

"It's fine. I'm going back to sleep."

Maria joined him, never removing the robe.

~ * ~

Early morning, Alex woke and, putting his hand on her back, said, "Good morning."

Maria groaned. "What time is it?"

Alex reached over and lowered the top of her bathrobe, exposing her shoulders; he kissed her neck and pushed her gently so she would face him. She resisted and took off her bathrobe to reveal she was naked beneath the terrycloth; she laid down on her stomach so quickly he couldn't see her front in the dim light. Alex swung his leg over her, settling gently below her buttocks. He rubbed her back, lowering his hands from her shoulders down her spine. Sliding down her legs, he massaged from her upper thighs to her ankles. Maria lifted slightly from her knees, and Alex entered her. They'd formed a rhythm that left them both satisfied and momentarily tired. Afterward, Maria stayed on her stomach, moving her head to the side.

"Why don't you shower first, and I'll get breakfast," she said.

Before going into the bathroom, he looked back and saw she was still on her stomach.

When Alex entered the kitchen, he poured coffee while Maria placed scrambled eggs on two plates.

She said between sipping coffee. "I promised we would have the day together yesterday, and I didn't come through. I cleared my calendar for today, deputized my assistant, and except for possibly a few phone calls, I'm free all day."

Late morning, they drove to Salinas, an agricultural region where strawberries, lettuce, tomatoes, and spinach dominated, passing fields watered by perforated pipes between the rows.

In the afternoon, they traveled to old missions in the surrounding area before returning and having dinner at a restaurant. After returning, they watched a movie, sitting on the couch, Maria leaning into Alex. At times, she looked up and kissed him; some were prolonged. He put his hands under her blouse and rubbed her back, and she settled closer. Unfastening her blouse to move his hand unimpeded down her spine, he circled to her sides and toward her front.

She sat up abruptly and switched her position, and her body was across his lap; she threw her arms around his neck and pressed her lips against his. The movie continued, but they left the room and went toward her bedroom. The fading sun was still pushing light under the blinds, and Maria led him toward the east-facing spare bedroom. The room was even darker than her bedroom. She stopped outside the door, said she wanted to change, and ran to her bedroom, returning quickly, covered by a pale blue t-shirt. They made love slowly, and both stared at the ceiling at the end.

Maria purred, "So good."

Alex sat up. "Maria, we've been intimate three times, and you've never removed the damn t-shirt. You keep the other rooms well-lit, but the bedrooms are dark. I'm unclear why we came into this room instead of your bedroom. You're not shy; you've never been with me. I have to envision your breasts from memory."

"I get chilly, and I like making love in the dark. Besides, I don't want you to be disappointed." She wasn't looking at him.

"Maria, don't take offense, but that's bullshit. I haven't been with you long this time, but I don't believe you lack confidence in your body." He got up from the bed and stood near her, still naked. "Do you think I'm proud of this body? We're older; it happens and much less to you."

Her voice rose. "You think you know me so well after a few days?"

"I'm not trying to start an argument, but I think you're keeping something from me."

Alex watched as she put on the bedside lamp and, closing her eyes, lifted the T-shirt. Alex could see the surgery marks on the right breast area and the difference in size between the two. She was crying.

"I had breast cancer and treatment, which included chemotherapy. The physicians can do wonders with reconstructive surgery, but not completely."

"You are no less beautiful, nor is your body any less appealing."

"Don't patronize me, Alex. I'm different, not just there," she put her hand over her breast. "When I was first diagnosed, I went into a tailspin, went through a range of emotions, stopped painting, and avoided friends, afraid I could die, or cancer would return, afraid people would look at me differently. After surgery, I never showed the scars to a lover. You don't feel whole or normal when a piece of you is removed and you're left with a deformity."

He removed her hand, bent over, and kissed her breast. "Please don't cover it up again."

"Should I walk around topless as well as barefoot?" Maria said—her mood was lifting.

"Fine with me," he answered, smiling.

The banter changed as Maria cried again. "Wearing a t-shirt with only panties beneath made me feel young and sexy before I got sick. Lately, I've been putting oversized pajamas to bed, fooling myself that I didn't need intimacy and could go without sex. You were nearly my first sexual experience when we were young, and now the first in a long while. You could also be my last as the herd thins, or I lose interest."

"Don't make assumptions."

Nine

The next night, the bedside lamp was on; they held each other for a long time, dozing at times, waking only to tighten the hold until late at night, the embrace turned into lovemaking, without a t-shirt.

"You're pretty virile for an old guy," she said as they leaned back.

"And out of practice. But it's like—"

Maria punched his arm.

"Ouch; what was that for?"

"You were going to say it's like riding a bicycle. Not the best analogy."

Alex smiled and squeezed her shoulders.

In the morning, Alex rose early and saw the other side of the bed was empty. Walking into the kitchen, he noticed a note leaning against an empty coffee cup; further down the table, bagels were lined up alongside a stick of butter on a small plate. He read the note, which said she was getting dressed in the other bedroom to avoid waking him, and she had to go to the gallery early. Alex was biting into a cinnamon bagel when she entered the kitchen. Maria wore a pink blouse, black skirt, and low heels. Kissing him on top of the head, she said, "I shouldn't be long, probably back before you showered and dressed if you move slow."

In an exaggerated movement of her hips, she walked toward the front door and turned her head, displaying a coy smile before she twisted the knob. Slowly finishing the doughy bagel and gulping down two cups of coffee, Alex entered the bathroom to get ready. He'd showered and shaved, and Maria hadn't returned. An hour later, she rushed in, repeating an apology until Alex assured her it wasn't necessary.

"I'm going to change into jeans, and we can go."

"Go where?"

"We're driving north on Route One, at least to Big Sur. It's a fabulous and unnerving ride; you'll see. I'll drive so you can enjoy the view. Bring your cell phone."

"Why—" He stopped when he saw her phone on the coffee table.

They headed south to the edge of Monterey into Carmel and onto Highway 1, which ran along the Santa Lucia mountains; the concrete road was close to the steep coastal cliffs and ascended to such a height that Alex felt they were riding into low clouds. The highway was unprotected by guardrails; the cliffs dropped straight down into the churning ocean. In one section of the road, an open-spandrel arch bridge crossed a stretch of sea that had cut into the mountains. "They named it: Bixby Bridge," Maria said as they crossed the structure. "I hope you're not afraid of heights."

"It's scary from this side of the car, but beautiful. I could say that about you, as well."

"I'll take the beautiful part, but why scary?"

"Before and now—recognizing we've had only a short time together—I've sensed so much going on in your head, I don't know. I've wondered, for example, would you have told me about your illness and surgery if we hadn't made love and I hadn't pressed? You tried to shield the scars from me."

"Probably not. Alex, I never know when you've had enough of this area, of me. How can I share, or have you mean more to me, knowing you're going back east one day? I said earlier I wouldn't think about that, but it's gotten harder."

"When I was young, I thought life would get simpler in my later years, but I'm more uncertain, more confused than ever; too much has happened in my life. I can't be concerned with endings or with leavings. But I'll not leave from here because I'm tired of this place, and certainly not because I've tired of you."

"I'd lean over and kiss you, but I might let go of the wheel, and we'd go over the cliff."

They traveled further to where the road descended, and small stretches of beach were close to the highway. At Big Sur, they pulled off and found a restaurant where they could eat outdoors. They sat side by side on the bench seats. After eating, they walked down a section of sand and looked out at the ocean.

"Have you ever painted the view from the highway or here?" Alex asked.

"Yes, of the ocean from Highway One, but it's abstract. There are so many fine photographs of the scenery, so I wanted to capture the fog, the rawness of the cliffs, and the waves pounding against the rock edges, wearing away the earth."

Alex put his arm around Maria, she reached around his waist, and they stayed motionless, listening to the waves die against the stone or slap the sand.

They planned their next trip on the ride back— driving south to Santa Barbara.

"I'll need to buy more clothes," Alex said, "never having packed for this much time away."

"Tomorrow we explore the practical places: a great men's shop in town, the local cleaner, markets selling gifts you can send to your daughters. When you were in my gallery, you saw my displayed works; I'd like you to view the paintings I'm working on or keeping stored for the time being."

As soon as they entered her house, Maria kissed him, at first affectionately and soon seductively. They rushed toward the bedroom, leaving a trail of clothes to the door. While they hurried, her cell phone rang twice. Maria stopped at the entrance to her room and shut the door. After they made love, she said, "I'm hungry."

"Is that your idea of a post-coital statement?"

"Sorry, but I am, and also satisfied. I'll order takeout from an Italian restaurant nearby. The menu is in the kitchen." Maria got up and walked toward the kitchen. Alex unconsciously moaned. Maria turned her head and said, "You always liked my ass."

Staying in bed, they looked over the menu; Maria called with their selections. Leaning back, settling against Alex, she said, "Who's going to answer the door when our food arrives?"

"If I answer like this, I'll get less of a reaction than you would."

"Aha, you assume a man will bring the package. Sexist!"

"I'll get dressed," Alex said.

They ate and drank from a wine bottle she had opened at the table, their meals still in the tin containers.

"Your phone rang twice before we were barely in your room; did you hear it?"

"I didn't look at the message and shut the phone off."

"Maria, I appreciate the attention and time you've given me, but I don't expect you to pause your life. I told you that."

"It's the way I am. When I start a canvas, I become consumed, forgetting to eat and barely sleeping. I can be that way about other things."

"But couldn't those calls be important? You have an active career and business."

"First thing tomorrow, I'll listen to the messages, return calls, and go to the gallery, but you should go with me. You can see my uncompleted works, and some I still hold back."

The following day, they woke at the same time, and embraced until Alex broke first. "We should get dressed."

As they drove, Maria said little. When they pulled up in front of the gallery, Alex asked, "What are you thinking about; you've been distracted since breakfast."

She stopped the car, turned the ignition key, and looked at him. "I suspected the calls last night and the messages were about a showing in San Francisco. As a local artist, receiving an offer to be part of such a major display is an honor and a curse. Being respected in your part of the state can lead to bigger opportunities across the state and beyond."

Pausing to measure his reaction, she continued, "Recently, I was signed to be a part of a prestigious show in Frisco, including events, dinners, and parties where the best critics, wealthy collectors, and writers from major publications attend. A cable network is filming a special program at the gathering."

He sighed. "I can see where this is heading."

"It's going to take a lot of my time. I enjoy being with you, Alex and I dread the lost time together, but—"

"I understand, and I've said several times, you need to concentrate on your career, not me."

"There were years I believed my career was over; survival was my only focus. I couldn't paint or even look at my completed paintings. Now things are opening up for me. I feel motivated and inspired."

"I can keep myself busy, and we'll have the evenings."

"Not all of them." She lowered her head. "Any event like this requires planning, and the artists and the organizers need to coordinate what will be displayed. You can't miss being part of the process. Artists want the wall spaces that best highlight their works, so you must aggressively pursue visibility. The first meeting, including dinner and party, will be this weekend."

"I'll find things to do; don't worry about me."

"Like flirting with young women at the supermarket?"

They went inside, and she was greeted by her assistant, Becky, whose look of relief was evident. For about ten minutes, Becky read off phone calls and emails that had come while Maria had been ignoring all communication. Looking dismayed, the young woman shrugged and turned to Alex. He knew the reason for her dismay; Maria wasn't listening.

"Give me a few minutes; I want to show Alex some of my paintings upstairs."

The upper room was colored by spattered paint, and half-squeezed tubes were lined up on a small table, staining the wood with various hues. The ceiling was slanted, so the walls were the predominant section of the room. Sunlight peeked over the high-window ledges, and the angled light illuminated the paintings resting on the bare floor. An easel stood at the room center, and a nearly finished artwork was at the center of the frame. Alex saw the painting was a replica of the view from Highway 1. The fog gave the scene a shrouded quality, as if the mist extended from the coast to the edge of the horizon.

"The painting is beautiful," he said. "I didn't mind the steep drops from the highway, but when we encountered the fog, I felt as if we were climbing into the sky, losing a sense of the road's edge and the turn of the concrete beyond our view. You captured the image so well."

Maria smiled, approached, and kissed him. "The piece is nearly finished, but I'm selfishly reluctant to frame it and hang it downstairs."

Alex looked at the back of a small canvas next to the painting. Curious, he turned the artwork around and was surprised to see a replica of the large work.

"Do you always redo the same painting in a smaller version?"

Maria answered, "I do, but not often. Many artists sketch a subject as the prelude to the main piece. I prefer to create a miniature painting before deciding if I want to recreate it on a larger canvas."

"All these paintings are gorgeous. I'm hardly an art critic; I purchased most of the works on my office wall at a discount store."

She laughed. "Hopefully, you're developing an appreciation for art not found in the waiting rooms of dentists' offices. I hope now you'll buy artwork from the cliched, starving artists." Switching tone, she added, "Some people think art is a manual skill, but it's a visual ability. I based the painting on a foggy day, but my imagination extended the mist in my eyes. But emotion underlies all art, so the image also conveyed my mood."

"I hope you take the highway painting to the San Francisco show."

She looked at him. "I'm frightened; there is so much at stake. I wish you could come with me as my one-person cheering squad, but you would be sitting in a hotel room or wandering around the city until late at night."

They spent considerable time on the second level; Maria explained the background of scattered paintings. "Never having children, this is as close to a birthing room as I'll get. I love the smell of paint and turpentine."

Alex laughed. "The smells don't get you high, do they?"

"In some ways."

"We'd better get downstairs before Becky's blood pressure climbs further. I'll take the car, head back, and get some things I need from the stores. I suspect you'll be busy most of today. Call me when you want me to pick you up. We can go out for dinner."

She kissed him, and they headed downstairs. When Becky saw them, her eyes widened; "You're not leaving, are you, Maria?"

"Don't worry, Becky, just me." He stopped at the door, turned, and saw Maria and her assistant engaged in an animated conversation, Becky pointing toward a clipboard.

He drove around with no destination, arriving at her house an hour later. He entered the living room and settled on a gray chair underneath a window.

Clouds had taken over the sky; bright rain-empty stratocumulus clouds showed lacerations where sunshine rays escaped. He looked around the house and at the walls, noticing she didn't put her artwork on display as she'd told him in her bedroom one night.

Alex thought about the time he'd been spending with Maria and his hesitation—even the lack of consideration—about returning home. They had not discussed feelings toward each other or mentioned going home lately since the trip on Highway One.

Perhaps, he realized, he had missed the comfort of being in bed with a woman, making love, falling into a routine of at least temporary domesticity; they had not been part of his life for years. But he regretted how his presence was interfering with her focus on her career and artistry. As Maria promised, the region was beautiful, and there was much to explore. The area around where she lived was becoming familiar, losing a bit of awe.

Reaching into his pocket, he took out his cell phone and pressed the numbers.

"Dad," the voice on the phone said, "I was going to call you. What have you been doing since the last time we spoke? How are things going with Maria? When are—?"

"Wait, Bethany, one question at a time. I've mostly been sightseeing, plus the usual stuff, going out for dinner and running errands. Nothing necessarily exciting. Maria and I spend a lot of time together; as I told you in a prior call, I'm staying at her house."

"You have your own bedroom?" the question had a teasing tone. Alex's response was silence.

Bethany continued: "The big question: when are you coming home? You've not been away this long with the others."

"I don't know when."

"Okay, let me rephrase the question: *are* you coming home?"

"Of course, why would you ask such a question?"

"Because I don't know what's going on with you, and I'm not talking about activities. If the trip was to satisfy a curiosity about a woman from your past, you've probably accomplished that. I don't know your feelings about this woman; all I know is that you are distracted and upset after each trip. What will you be like now? Your other daughter has the same questions."

Alex answered, "This is the first time I've had to reflect on those same questions, so I don't have answers. All I know is I enjoy being with Maria and sharing her life, which is much different from mine. I'd talked at length about the meetings with Carolyn and Maddy, and will do so about Maria with you and Merry upon returning, just not now."

They continued their conversations, discussing other topics: her boyfriend, graduate school selection, and Merry. Bethany assured him she was keeping an eye on the house and stayed overnight once to ensure everything was working correctly.

Ten

The days passed quickly. Before Maria would travel, she returned home carrying takeout Chinese food. They were quiet as they ate until Maria reached across the table and grabbed Alex's hand.

"I should be so excited about going to San Francisco, but I'm sad."

"I'll miss you, too," he said, putting his hand over hers.

"I'm traveling early; please stay in bed. It'll be hard enough."

Maria called when she arrived at the hotel and again that night. She told him what was going on in San Francisco.

"I've met many influential people and other artists. I brought several pieces, and we had an informal showing of everyone's works. You were right; the highway painting received a lot of compliments. This evening we're having dinner and a party afterward and I wish you were here.

"Are you keeping yourself busy? I tell people you are my muse; you have encouraged me, and I suspect it shows. As much as I'm enjoying the activity, I miss you and am glad to know when I return home, you will still be there."

"I miss you, too."

"Alex, I need to forewarn you that when I get back, I'll need to be busy preparing for what's been called 'the main event,' I hope you will be patient and stay."

"I have no plans to leave."

"Please say it differently: I'm not leaving."

After he hung up, Alex ordered a takeout dinner and drove to the restaurant, picking up a bottle of wine before collecting the meal. Sitting on the couch, he ate from the metal container and sipped from the wineglass, glancing at a movie while thoughts swirled in his mind. In bed, he flipped through an art magazine from her nightstand until his eyes closed. Alex was startled from sleep by the house phone ringing nearby. Looking across the bed, he saw Maria's number appear on the telephone. The clock next to the phone read one fifteen.

Maria apologized for waking him and described the night's event, her voice high-pitched. Alex suspected she was mildly drunk. He listened until she finished and said he was glad she was having a good time. Before hanging up, Maria added that more activities were planned, and she wouldn't be home until late. Afterward, Alex tossed in the wide bed until falling asleep hours later.

In the morning, the sirens of police cars in a nearby neighborhood woke Alex; the sun lifted above the clouds lingering on the horizon after the early morning fog had faded. He dressed, ate breakfast, and drove to Carmel.

After parking, he walked around town and found most stores and restaurants were clustered around Ocean Avenue and the surrounding streets. As he passed the markets and places to eat, Alex noticed the storefronts were free of markings, the sidewalks were swept, and extended awnings were in vivid colors. Menus were behind clear glass on the building front. He thought of the touristy areas near his home;

many showed wear and mild disarray and storefront signs were often hand-drawn and fading from the weather.

He missed home and the familiar, flawed places, more real than towns like Carmel. The weather was mild, and he knew cold had stripped the trees at home. Once as he strolled, his cell phone rang and looking at it, he saw Maria's number appear but soon drop off. He considered calling her back and decided against it.

While dozing on the couch, Alex heard the front door open, and before he could say or do anything, Maria charged to where he was, nearly leaped on him, and kissed him. He gently touched her shoulders and moved her beside him. She smiled and drew closer to kiss him again, and he could smell alcohol on her breath.

"You took a big risk driving."

She ignored his comment. "I have wonderful news, but I can wait."

Maria got to her feet, grabbed Alex's hands, yanked him up, and pulled him to the bedroom. They made love, still partially dressed, until she fell back wearily against the pillow.

Alex got up to shut off the lights in the living room and lock the front door; when he returned, he saw Maria fully undressed, tucked under the blanket, and fast asleep. In the morning, he woke first and went into the kitchen. After making coffee, he brought a cup into the bedroom.

Maria reached the filled cup and brought the hot liquid to her mouth, smacking her lips. "I have a headache," she said.

Alex went into the bathroom and came out with two aspirins. "You were drunk last night."

"Not so drunk," she said coyly.

"Are you going to tell me the wonderful news?"

"Give me time to shower and get dressed. We can sit in the living room, and I'll tell you everything."

Maria wore a loose sweater, the sleeves pushed to just below her elbows. Standing, she would periodically pull at the stretched ends of the wool to cover her hands before folding her arms.

She sat next to him. "I've been offered a partnership with a known gallery in San Francisco. I will add my works and the paintings of other artists from surrounding areas. Of course, I will keep my studio and gallery downtown and continue to paint locally, but I will probably spend much more time north. This arrangement could be unfair to you, but we can work it out. After all, I won't be that far away."

Alex said nothing for a few minutes, and Maria stared at his eyes as if the pupils might reveal his thoughts.

"We should be celebrating," he said.

Maria kissed him. "Good plan. How about we spend the day together here, no trips or playing tourist, and tonight we can go to a great restaurant in town. My treat."

They decided on a picnic in the backyard with a blanket spread on the lawn at lunchtime and dined on sandwiches and lemonade she carried out in a basket. They heard the house phone ring. Maria got up and went inside to answer, staying for about ten minutes.

Apologizing, she offered to let any other calls go to message. "I left my cell inside. If you want to frisk me, go ahead." Alex leaped toward her, pushed her back on the blanket, and searched her pockets, allowing his hands to roam over her body until she interrupted him with a prolonged kiss. Soon, they rose to go into the house. Alex reached down to grab the basket, and she told him to leave it.

The restaurant had a wood-paneled interior with tables spread about the polished floor. Conic overhead lights illuminated the pressed white tablecloths, and waiters dressed in tuxedos ambled around the room carrying trays or taking orders. As soon as Alex and Maria were seated, a smiling, dark-haired woman approached their table and introduced herself as the sommelier, asking about their preferences and offering suggestions. Maria spoke more about the San Francisco trip and plans during dinner.

"There's so much to work out, and I have some ideas." She continued explaining her thoughts on how arrangements could be handled.

"If I'm going to spend a lot of time up there, maybe I can rent an apartment, and you can stay there with me."

Without responding to her idea, Alex asked questions about her trip.

Maria grabbed the check and placed her credit card on top. When they returned home, Alex went into the bedroom to hang his jacket, and Maria wasn't there when he returned to the living room. Still, the scraping sound of a chair moving along the hardwood floor drew his attention to a small room off to the side, where he found Maria typing on a laptop. Placing his hands on her shoulders, he asked what she was doing, and Maria explained she was jotting down some ideas.

"I'm going to bed," Alex said. Turning her head slightly, she responded, "Okay."

~ * ~

In the morning, Alex came down and saw Maria sitting at the table biting into a cream cheese-smothered bagel. She was wearing a short dress and high heels. Rising when he came closer, she put her arms around him and said, "It was nice just having time together. Now I have to focus on the gallery in town for part of the day. I'll be back as soon as I can."

Maria didn't return until early evening. Alex sat on the back porch and watched the day's last light fade, and heard Maria's car pull into the driveway. When she saw him coming near, she shrugged and said, "I'm sorry; it took a lot longer than I thought."

Alex kissed her and said, "Don't apologize for having to work long hours. You have a demanding job on the creative side and the business aspect on the other."

They walked into the house with their arms around each other. As soon as she stepped inside, she smelled the cooking. "You're making fish—great." At dinner, they discussed her day until Maria said, "We're always talking about my life; what happened today for you, besides making a great dinner? Have you talked to Merry or Bethany? I'd love to meet them one day." She spoke so fast the sentences were running together.

Alex answered he'd not spoken to his daughters recently. They entered the kitchen with the plates and utensils, putting them in the dishwasher. When done, Maria put her arms around his neck and said, "I want to make love to you, but I wouldn't be as energetic; I'm tired. My god, we're getting like an old married couple."

"Damn it," Alex said, "Stop apologizing for everything, just like you need to stop asking me about leaving. If you have to work late, fine, or don't want to have sex, it's fine, too."

"Have sex? Hmm. We'll *have sex* tomorrow, or maybe you can just fuck yourself."

At breakfast, Maria breathed in and said, "I won't apologize again, but I need to explain. You traveled all this distance, and I haven't spent as much time as I'd like with you. But more importantly, I miss being with you. My biggest fear is that I'll come home one day and find a note on the table. I've been alone a lot lately, and it's been wonderful to have someone."

Alex reached across the table and touched her hand. Before leaving the table, she added, "Please don't use those words for what we have and do."

He knew what she meant.

Alex tried to reach Bethany, and when she didn't answer, he left a message on her cell phone. He contacted Merry on her house phone, and neither daughter had returned his call by late afternoon. Maria returned home, and he explained how he had been unsuccessful in reaching his daughters.

"They're busy women, and I'm sure they'll get back to you."

While she went into the bedroom to change, Alex's phone rang.

"Hello, Merry," he chirped.

"Dad, Dad, something bad has happened." She was crying.

"Is it Bethany?" His voice rose.

"No, it's Bradley, her boyfriend. He was in an accident." Merry paused and breathed in. "He's in critical condition, and Bethany is so distraught, as you can imagine. I went to the hospital to be with her and the surgeon said Bradley may not get through the next few days. I'm worried about him and my sister. She loves him very much. They have been hopeful about their plans and are discussing getting married."

Alex's eyes filled. "I'm getting the next flight home and will telephone you with the details. I've been trying to reach Bethany."

"She mentioned you called, but said she didn't want you to rush home and leave Maria. There was nothing you could do. If Bethany talks to you, she'll break down trying to be strong. I'm sure you'll hear from her soon."

They spoke longer, and when he hung up, Alex turned and saw Maria standing behind him.

"What is it, Alex? I see you're upset."

He explained the call, and she hugged him. "What can I do?" she asked.

Alex said he had to leave and needed her help to call for a flight.

"I can contact my travel agent first thing in the morning, and she can scan the airlines' schedules for the earlier and most direct flights from San Francisco."

Alex felt exhausted and told Maria he was going to bed. He undressed, lifted the cover, and slid under the sheet. Before he could settle, Maria slipped into the other side of the bed, leaned across, and held him.

Alex spoke, "I'm sorry I was so short with—"

Maria gently put her hand over his mouth. "We'll talk in the morning."

When Alex came downstairs the next morning, he saw Maria pacing.

"You were up early," Alex said.

"Who said I even slept? Let's sit on the couch so we can talk."

Maria looked at him. "I know you need to hurry home." She paused before continuing, her voice cracking, "and I know you won't be coming back. I think the possibility that we won't have as much time together as we hoped and wanted is getting to the both of us.

"What can you do while I'm gone for long stretches? This is not your home here. We live on opposite sides of the country, and your life is too attached to the East Coast and mine in California. I could love you, Alex, but the time has never been right for us. When we were young and now. I always knew but wouldn't accept it; I kept questioning you about leaving because I feared being alone and without you.

"The accolades I received, especially lately, have bolstered my artistic confidence; you have restored faith in myself as a woman. But I can't turn down this opportunity or attempt it part-time. The visibility will benefit me more than my paintings. I can also display and promote interest in artists from the Monterey area, people I know are capable artists and my friends. I fooled myself into thinking we could make it work and live in this town and San Francisco. I imagined everything would have been perfect, but that was unrealistic. I could sense your restlessness. I need to do more in my life, and so do you. It just can't be here or with me."

Alex didn't respond. "I'd better get ready," he said after a long silence.

He packed while Maria made the flight arrangements. She convinced him to eat while explaining the schedule to the East Coast. "You'll fly out of the Monterey airport to San Francisco for a direct flight home. I want to go with you to the airport in your car, and after you drop off the rental, I'll stay with you for a while. I'll call a friend to pick me up or take a cab home when you board. I want to be with you as long as I can. Alex, you have said nothing about what I told you about us."

"Maria, my head is spinning from what you said and what's happening at home. I think you're right, but I can't stand the thought of losing you."

Alex loaded his suitcases into the trunk of the car. During the short drive to the Monterey airport, he joked he'd bought so many clothes locally he could barely pack everything. After returning the rental, they went inside the terminal, and Alex confirmed his schedule and waited to load his bags.

While still in the waiting area, Maria said, "I'll leave you here. I can't watch you go to the gate or see the plane take you away. I will never forget you, Alex. This has been—"

Alex held her, and they kissed before he walked toward the gate.

Alex had to wait in San Francisco for an hour for the next flight. He realized he hadn't contacted Merry with his arrival time, but as he hit the numbers on his phone, he saw a text from her.

He called and apologized. "I'll be home in—"

"Maria called me and gave me your flight details. She figured you could forget with the rush to leave. She copied my number from your cell. Maria seems lovely and upset. We can talk about it much later. I'll pick you up at the airport, and we can go to the hospital directly."

~ * ~

Alex embraced his daughter at the terminal, and after picking up his suitcases, they headed to the hospital. Merry gave him the latest update on Bradley's condition during the ride.

At the hospital, father and daughter walked down the hallway to the critical care section. In the distance, they saw Bethany running to them; she embraced her father, sobbing as she held him. He threw his arms around her, and they stayed in the embrace until Bethany stepped back and squeezed her sister's hand. The smell of disinfectant filled the space, and the paging speakers announced names and notices frequently.

"He's a little better," Bethany said. "His parents just left." The three sat together, often in silence, waiting for an update on Bradley's condition. Finally, Alex spoke up.

"Honey, I bet you haven't eaten today and likely little yesterday. Why don't we get something to eat? I saw a restaurant just outside the hospital. We won't be gone long."

When Bethany nodded, Merry took her hand, and they left. At the restaurant, Alex asked more about the accident, and Bethany explained what had occurred between her tears. "It wasn't his fault. The other driver was arrested."

They returned to the hospital and took the stairs to the ICU; Alex checked with the nurse for any news about Bradley, and the sisters saw the nurse shake her head. After a few hours, Alex offered to stay while the two of them went to his house to rest. "The hospital is closer to home than where either of you lives. We'll stand by in shifts. I'll stay for the night."

When they were all back and waiting in the morning, a doctor came over to them and explained Bradley had shown improvement overnight but was still unconscious. He looked at Bethany and said, "your husband," when speaking to her.

Alex and Merry stared at Bethany after the doctor left.

"Bradley's parents told the doctors and nurses I was his wife so I could stay with him and get reports of his condition. They're wonderful people and know how much I love him. His folks will be here soon, and you can meet them. I should call them with the latest report."

She took out her cell phone and walked a short distance down the hall. By late afternoon, Alex had met Bradley's parents, who offered to stay into the evening, mentioning they were in a nearby hotel and Bethany could remain in an adjacent room they would pay for. Merry told her father she'd taken off a few days and would stay at his house. Before they went home, Alex ordered pizza, and they watched a mystery movie on television. Around three a.m., Alex was awakened by the ringing phone.

"Dad! He's conscious; I spoke to him." Her voice was wavering. Bethany then said, "You don't have to come up today. You've had a long flight and an experience on the West Coast. The nurse had a portable bed put into Bradley's room. Remember, I'm his wife. I didn't have to stay with his folks. They'll be here soon and will go home if assured Bradley is out of the woods."

Walking to where Merry was sleeping, Alex opened the door a crack and saw she was breathing deeply. He waited until daybreak to share the news.

Disregarding Bethany's suggestion, Alex and Merry went to the hospital late in the morning and met with Bethany. Bradley was talking, but his appearance took Alex aback. His face was swollen, bandages were wrapped around his head, and his left arm was in a sling. Monitors beeped rhythmically.

A nurse came in, looked at the chart on the end of the bed, and smiled approvingly. A few hours later, Bradley said he was tired, and the three left the room.

In the hallway, Bethany said, "You both can go back to your lives. I'm staying for a few days. As soon as Bradley is well enough to leave the hospital, his father will come back, pick him up when he's discharged, and bring him to their house. I'll drive to the apartment, gather clothes, and will go to be with Bradley at his parents'."

Alex drove Merry to his house.

"I want to hear about your time in Monterey and Maria, but now I need to be with my husband. I also have some work to do before returning to the office."

Alex went inside to an empty house. He answered the doorbell, and a delivery man handed him a thin, wrapped package. Taking it into the kitchen, he cut the string and tore off the brown wrapping paper. Inside was the small painting of the highway along the ocean's edge. He wept over all that had happened.

Part 4

Eleven

"How is Dad?" Bethany asked her sister.

"He seems as if he's struggling, is at loose ends. Months have passed since he saw Maria, and sometimes I think he's waiting for her call, just by the way he jumps toward the house phone when it rings, and he never lets his cell out of sight when I saw him last. Right now, he's painting the living room and doing minor repairs. Maybe he's planning to sell the house; with you leaving for graduate school in the fall, the house is too big for one person. Maybe he's getting it ready for your wedding," she added coyly.

"I wish to hell he hadn't started the whole search for women from his past. But maybe with that all out of his system, he'll look ahead. I also wonder if he regrets selling his business. He's too young to be whittling on the porch. What's he going to do now?" Bethany added, "Has he talked about Maria to you?"

"No. I've been to see him after he returned from California, and he gave me what I would call a summary. I have many questions, but he said he needs more time. I've not pushed the issue further."

"I spoke to him on the phone too, and he said even less when I tried to probe."

"He said he called Maria to let her know he was home and they talked at length. A few days later, he contacted her again and they even discussed his traveling back to California and giving the relationship more time, but they decided against it. Dad's hurting and I suspect she is, too." Merry paused before changing the subject. "Speaking of plans, how is Bradley, and are you both going to grad school?"

"He's recovering well. We're back to school, and our professors have understood about our time out of class; our scholarships aren't in jeopardy. Over the summer, Bradley and I will get married and maybe take a brief honeymoon just before going to our new university, look for someplace to stay, and scout for jobs. I admit his injury made me think more about being with him as husband and wife. He'll be fully healed and able to work, perhaps in the university. Bradley is good with his hands." Bethany paused. "I know what you're thinking; that's not what I meant." She heard Merry laughing.

"Are you visiting Dad soon?" Merry asked.

"Yes, this weekend. I appreciate the time you've been spending with him while I've been with Bradley in his recovery."

"The time together has provided an opportunity to get closer to him."

"I have to go to the pharmacy to pick up Bradley's medication; we'll speak soon."

Merry paused. "Bethany, can you stay on—I want to talk to you about something."

"Of course. Is everything okay?"

"Yes, it's wonderful. I think I'm pregnant!"

Bethany had to pull the phone away from her ear. "That means I'm going to be an aunt."

Merry laughed. "And I'm going to be a mother."

"I have so many questions, like due date, boy or a girl."

"Wait! My gynecologist hasn't confirmed the pregnancy, but I'm pretty certain."

"Have you told Dad?"

"No, and I won't until my physician confirms; Dad has had a lot of disappointment, and I don't want to add to it if I'm wrong. I've not told anyone except my husband and you."

"The news will make him happy, but you are right; the letdown would be poorly timed if you aren't expecting. By the way, Bethany is a good name for a girl?"

"No way! One Bethany in my life is enough. I love you, sis."

As soon as she hung up, Bethany woke Bradley, who was napping. "You're going to be an uncle."

~ * ~

Alex used a roller on the walls leaving blue paint on the drop cloth and a thin line of color on the ceiling. Stepping off the ladder, he walked a few feet back, looked at the partially completed wall and said to himself, "Maria wouldn't appreciate my artwork."

He recalled admitting to his older daughter in their latest visit he missed Maria and hadn't fully processed what had happened.

"The closeness began almost immediately. I stayed at a motel and before long, was in her house and sharing her bed. Maria was damaged by prior failed relationships, physically injured by cancer, and was emerging from a struggle to revive her artistic career.

"She is courageous and determined, but as our relationship grew, her professional opportunities expanded quickly. As hard as she tried to carve out days for us to be together, the pulls on her time were taking over. Maria said she was holding back emotionally, but I'm not sure.

"I can't get past the irony: her career was blossoming, and mine was over, yet we were nearly the same age. Timing is everything, as they say. I'm not in the right frame of mind to question the value of meeting with the three women of my past; except for Carolyn, the leaving was hurtful. I don't know what I've learned from all this-there must be a lesson there somewhere I'll eventually discover."

His daughter listened attentively and without question, but at the end of his openness, she said, "Maybe Carolyn could be a respite from the pain of the others. Why not call her but let some time go by first. You're in too fragile a state for another disappointment."

Holding the brush and staring at the partially covered wall, he smiled, thinking how perceptive his elder daughter had become. He was certain she shared their conversation with Bethany.

By evening, the room was completed, and he made dinner. Pouring wine in his glass, he thought about the three women as if constructing a column list of comparisons.

The time with Carolyn had been the sweetest, with no disagreements or conflicting emotions. With Maddy, there was the sense of a mounting, prohibited relationship, and a near betrayal paused by momentary guilt. With Maria, there was the competition for her attention and commitment, a thwarted love, and a satisfying intimacy now ended.

How do you compare three distinctive involvements and three different women? But what was common? They were all confident women, had thriving careers, and were open about their feelings. What could he have done differently?

He realized for two: Maddy and Maria, nothing. Both women were at a critical point in their lives—Maddy in her marriage and Maria in her career. He had only complicated their lives, capitalizing on a prior relationship to restore some part of what they once had. There had never been any certainty that a relationship from years ago would have been successful now. He kept going back to the same point: the volatility, the anguish, and the lingering emotional exhaustion were present with two of the three. Was it because he didn't have the same feelings toward Carolyn, or did the heartbreak over Maddy and Maria smother any attachment with Carolyn or further interest of reconnecting with her again?

The nights are longer now, he thought, since leaving Maria. He was awake and getting ready to paint the bedrooms—Merry's room to start. When the family moved into the house, the sisters fought over the bedrooms. Merry, who was nine, asked her parents for a tape measure and, stretching the tape, claimed her stake based on the differences in inches and on her older age. Bethany sulked through dinner but soon accepted the room assignments, Alex recalled. His cell phone rang. Retrieving the cell from the other room and saying hello, Alex was momentarily taken aback. "Carolyn, it's good to hear from you."

"I haven't spoken to you for a while. How are you?" she asked. After Alex answered, she continued, "I'm calling because I'm going to be in your area and was wondering if you'd have time for dinner the night I arrive."

"I'd love to see you again. When are you arriving?"

"A week from Friday. My niece is getting married, and the reception is about ten miles south of your town."

"Are you sure your boyfriend wouldn't mind? I recall you told me you were seeing someone."

"The relationship was never serious, and now it's non-existent."

"Who will be your plus one for the reception?"

"I'm going solo."

"I have an idea: I'll be your date for the reception, and you can tell people who ask that I'm an old friend."

"Alex, that's gracious, but I don't want to impose. I'm sure you have a lot to do."

He laughed. "I'm painting the bedrooms and later the kitchen. I welcome a reason to break away from the fumes and tedious tasks."

"Is there any reason why you're painting the house? Most people take on that project when they're planning to sell."

"My daughters tell me I should consider selling—the house is too big for one person now that both have moved away."

"Your older is married, isn't she, and the younger going to graduate school? Did I remember correctly?"

"Yes, you did. Bethany still lives here but is at school most weekends. The latest change, however, is that she is getting married before graduate school. But simply, the current coat on the walls is over ten years old and shows the wear. Plus, it keeps me busy."

"I'm looking forward to seeing you," Carolyn said.

When they hung up, he walked around Merry's bedroom, twirling a dry paint brush as if leading a band.

On Thursday evening, he was watching television when his cell phone rang. Carolyn was on the line.

"What's going on in your region?" she asked, frustration showing in her tone. "As I mentioned in our last conversation, I was driving to your area, staying overnight at a nearby hotel, going to a reception on Saturday, and leaving on Sunday. I can't get a hotel or anything within a reasonable distance. The receptionist at one place I called said there is some sort of big convention in town. I won't have time to see you on Friday, and I'll have to leave the event earlier than I hoped. If you don't want to go with me on Saturday, I'll understand. Shit! I'm angry at myself for not making arrangements sooner."

For a few seconds, Alex didn't speak. "I have an idea. Why don't you stay at my place? We can still have dinner on Friday, go to the reception the next day, and come back here for the second night. There are three bedrooms, at least one will be freshly painted, I might add. Carolyn, we're adults and can stay in the same house for two nights without assumptions or being concerned about perceptions."

"Alex, you're wonderful to offer—"

"Before you say no, I may want to sell at some point. I can use your expert opinion on how to prepare the house best. You'll be doing me a favor."

Carolyn's hesitancy remained apparent by her lack of response, Alex thought.

"We slept in the same room, remember. Here, you'll have a separate bedroom," Alex continued to rationalize.

Instead of directly agreeing, she said, "I won't ask about what happened with the other women."

"Okay; see you on Friday." Before hanging up, he gave her the address.

On the Friday she was arriving, he cleaned the house, changed the sheets in the bedroom, and stocked up on food. At about six, he heard a car slow near the home and stepped outside to see Carolyn pull up to the curb, and before she stopped, Alex waved for her to pull into the empty driveway. When she got out, Alex saw she was wearing a short skirt, tan coat, and flats. Her hair was longer than he remembered from the last time he had seen her. When she smiled at him, he felt as if the light over the garage door shifted and pointed toward her face, giving her a glow. Carolyn hugged him, and close up, he was reminded of her loveliness.

Alex broke the moment by asking about her luggage, and she answered by opening the truck from the release on her car keys. Heading inside, Carolyn took hold of his free arm and said, "I'm so grateful to you for everything. I'll pay for dinner."

Just inside the doorway, Alex said, "No need, I made dinner."

Carolyn stopped quickly and, still holding his arm, nearly caused him to drop the suitcase. "You cook?" She laughed. "I recall one time, many years ago, we were at my house early morning, and my parents were still sleeping; you volunteered to make me breakfast. You burned the eggs, and while you were panicking trying to rescue the charred yolk, you forgot about the bread in the toaster, and the smoke poured out, setting off the fire alarm."

Chuckling, he said, "You would remember that. My skills in the kitchen have greatly improved. The meal is nothing fancy."

Alex led her to the bedroom and put the suitcase on the floor. The room had a faint odor of paint. The double bed was in the center, and a nightstand was on the right side. A dresser leaned against the far wall.

"No pictures?" Carolyn said.

"I took them down, and in fact, the largely poster-dominated walls were one of the reasons I had to paint. This is Bethany's room I finished after we spoke. My daughter nailed something to the plasterboard to decide if it was positioned correctly, and if not, she made a new hole until the room looked like a pincushion when bare. Merry is the opposite: she measures first. That best defines their unique personalities."

"I'm impressed with your painting skills."

"Just don't look too closely. I'll give you time to settle and freshen up," he said, leaving the room.

He shook the pans over the stove's burner and checked on the chicken cooking in the oven. Carolyn came in, and turning to look at her, Alex said, "Could you open the wine. The glasses are in the cabinet to your left."

She poured the chardonnay and handed him one. They toasted by clinking glasses. For the rest of the evening, they talked about her job and other elements of both their lives. Carolyn remembered other aspects of their youthful relationship, stories of families, and how they grew apart once they started college. Alex got up from the table and walked to the CD player, sorted through a stack of music discs, and pushed one into the player. The first song that came out of the speakers caused Carolyn to smile.

"That was our song!"

"I bought it when I came back from seeing you."

They sat on the couch, saying nothing until Alex offered to make coffee. Carolyn said she would help with the dishes before the coffee, and they went into the kitchen and divided duties, he washing and she drying. Midway through the cleaning, Alex said, "You know I have a dishwasher."

"I do," she said coquettishly.

They had coffee at the table; Alex added brandy to each cup before filling it with the black brew. He reminded her they had a lot of time before the wedding, and he would show her the town and surrounding area, adding, "The region has changed a lot since you lived here."

Alex explained where towels were kept, and they both went to bed.

After sleeping late, Alex woke first, went into the kitchen, took out cereal boxes, and put them on the table. He was wearing pajamas and a bathrobe. A half-hour later, Carolyn came into the kitchen similarly dressed.

"Good morning," Alex said. "I took out boxes of cereal, and the milk is on the refrigerator door."

They sat across from each other, biting into the crunchy cereal.

"Alex, you don't have to drive to the wedding. I can pick you up, and we can go directly to the reception."

"I don't mind. I remember your sister, Ashley, although, after so many years, she'll probably not recognize me."

"Oh, she will. I told her you were going to be my date for the celebration. I once thought she'd had a crush on you in high school, but she'd never admitted it."

They were in no hurry and were surprised when the front door flew open and Bethany came in. She stopped abruptly and stared at her father and Carolyn.

Red-faced, she said, "I'm sorry; I didn't know you had a guest."

Alex introduced Carolyn, and Bethany blurted, "Oh, you're number—"

Carolyn smiled, shook hands with Bethany, and said, "One. I don't mind being first."

"I came home to get some lighter clothes now that the weather has warmed a bit."

"You're early; that's not typical of you."

"Bradley is going to physical therapy this afternoon, and I'm taking him." Looking at Carolyn, she explained, "Bradley's my boyfriend."

"I'm staying in your room, I believe. Why don't I quickly dress and be out of your way." With that, she left the kitchen.

As soon as Carolyn was out of view, Bethany leaned over and whispered to her father, "What's going on here?"

"I'm taking her to her niece's wedding reception, and she couldn't get a hotel room, so I offered."

Bethany laughed, but quickly covered her mouth. "I bet she ran into my room to mess the bed, so it looked like she slept there."

He knew the ribbing wouldn't stop.

"Dad, considering your recent activities, you should think about a vasectomy."

"I'm sure you're going to share all this with Merry."

"You bet, and appropriately embellished."

Bethany quieted when Carolyn came back. The two women spoke at length, Bethany asking about her father as a young man before going to her room to gather her clothes. After loading the car, she hugged Carolyn and took her father's arm, walking him to the front of her vehicle.

"Thanks for being nice to Carolyn," Alex said.

"She's delightful; besides, she could be my stepmother," her sides shook from holding in the laughter.

Alex embraced his daughter, and with his freed hand, softly smacked her butt.

Carolyn had left the kitchen by the time he went back inside; before she'd gone up, she'd cleared the table and put the plates and utensils in the sink. Alex and Carolyn regrouped in the living room, and as he'd promised, he took her around the area. They talked about reminiscences of places they'd been to when they were young, such as their high school and the local movie theater. They had lunch where they'd often dined and stopped at the grassy field where they'd stopped most often at night to embrace and kiss in the dimly lit parking lot. Arriving back at his house, they paused in the driveway, and Carolyn was the first to speak.

"That was a magical time in my life, and you were a big part of it. I rarely lament about getting older, but being here now and thinking back makes me smile and feel sad at the same time." She reached across and kissed him on the cheek. "Thanks for the tour of our old neighborhood and our past."

The wedding was at five, and they left his house in time for the service. The sky was clear, and the sun was on the decline, still radiating enough heat that heavy jackets weren't needed.

As they drove, Alex thought back to another event they attended—their prom. She had been in a pink gown, and he was wearing a tuxedo. Joining friends at the school gym, they'd danced, laughed, and sipped on the secretly spiked punch. He also recalled that on the ride home, she'd cried over the looming end of their high school years and the pending separation when they would start college in different states.

"Do you remember the summer before college—we spent as much time together as we could."

Carolyn smiled, "Yes, I do. We were on the edge of adulthood, about to experience the biggest change in our lives. My parents were fond of you but admitted to me later they'd feared we would 'stifle' each other—that's the word my father had used."

"I've learned long ago, but especially lately, that wondering *what if* is fruitless?"

They pulled into the church parking lot. Carolyn greeted people she knew and introduced Alex, except to Ashley, who smiled at seeing her sister's old boyfriend.

"I'm glad you came," Ashley said as she hugged him. She closely resembled her sibling, except that Ashley was heavier. "Isn't it strange that the last time the three of us were together, we were younger than our children?" Carolyn said.

Ashley took them to the section for family, and within minutes, the organ music keyed to start the procession down the aisle. Alex looked at Carolyn, and both were lost in their separate thoughts.

Afterward, the reception was in a large building festooned with white streamers and blue balloons. Cooking odors from the large kitchen permeated the open room; each table contained a placard with names posted on the cardboard strip. Former friends and distant relatives drew Carolyn's attention over the evening, and she looked apologetically at Alex. A cousin pulled Carolyn from her chair to say hello to her children just as the music started. Alex stayed seated and looked around the room at the other guests and the married couple on the dais when he felt a tug on his jacket. Carolyn was smiling, looking down at him. She said, "Can I have this dance?"

Moving to an empty space, Carolyn spun around, put her hand on his shoulder, and moved close to him. They danced to the song, and when the music ended, a similar slow beat followed, and Carolyn and Alex stayed connected. They sat at the table between time on the dance floor and Carolyn explained the family connection by discreetly pointing out other guests. Wine bottles were placed on each table, and diligent waitstaff replaced empties. The newly married couple had left before the end of the celebration; Alex rose near the end of the reception while the band was packing.

They agreed Alex should drive; on the way, Carolyn leaned against him, closing her eyes. Once inside the house, she perked up, and they poured from a wine bottle Alex opened.

"Alex, I said I wouldn't ask you about the other women, but I have been curious—"

He drew in a deep breath and talked about the visit with Maddy and Maria, pausing periodically. Carolyn was quiet, looking at him the whole time he spoke.

"I don't know what I learned from the whole—as my daughters called it—adventure or quest. What was my purpose and what does it say about me? Am I afraid of the future?"

"Sometimes," she said, "things just happen, and when you analyze the reasons, you miss the experience."

"Are you talking about us as well?"

"Right now, I'm just enjoying being with you; I don't think beyond that. Perhaps after I leave, I'll wonder."

"We should get together again soon," Alex said.

Carolyn paused, got up, and looked at Alex. Sitting back down, she said, "Do you realize how much we've touched each other, hugged and kissed platonically since we've been here and my town earlier. There were times when I think we both felt a little more than friendship. If we continue being in proximity in a private place—your house or mine—we may slip and do something unintended we can't take back. I can't be a friend with benefits. It's late and I'm tired; let's go to bed *separately*," she added, smiling.

In the morning, Carolyn woke early and was dressed before Alex came down.

"I have a busy week ahead and need to take it easy for a day, especially since I didn't sleep well last night. I shouldn't have asked you about the other women. I'd promised I wouldn't, but I was drunk enough to disregard my word. I hope you forgive me."

Alex responded, "I'm glad we spoke. I'm comfortable with you, I felt no restrictions. I try to explain what happened recently to my kids, but they don't understand fully."

Carolyn chortled. "I wish I'd been a fly on the wall when you told them about your time with me." She hugged him and said, "I should be going."

He walked her to her car, and they hugged again; he stayed by the driveway until she was out of sight.

~ * ~

Later in the day, the phone rang, and Alex, back to painting, went into the living room to answer. Merry was on the line.

"Dad, I want to see you on Saturday, assuming you'll be around and by yourself." She put her hand over her mouth to stifle a laugh.

"Okay, I gather you spoke to your sister, so I hope your visit isn't to pump me about Carolyn's visit."

"Bethany told me about your overnight guest, but you know how she exaggerates, and I wanted to get the straight scoop. Besides, that's not the only reason."

"Which you will not share with me before you arrive. I'm around, likely still painting, so you can bring old clothes and help."

"That may not be a good idea," she said, hanging up quickly before he asked what she meant.

Monday evening, Carolyn called. "I called because I was troubled about my last words on the day I left. We were good together—as friends; I want our relationship to continue without complexity."

"I'm glad to hear you say so. Losing you as a friend would be a shame. I enjoy your company, and while I've questioned the logic of going backward in time recently, you've been a total pleasure each time. Do you realize we've connected three times besides when we were very young: the reunion, the days I spent in your town and, of course, the wedding, all without discord or heartbreak? How could I not want to continue seeing you? I can travel to your area and stay in a hotel if need be."

"That's part of what I regret saying. We're adults, practically senior citizens," she added with a laugh. "You can stay at my place without us ripping each other's clothes off."

"Speak for yourself," he responded jokingly. "Let's plan for me to come there. Merry is coming here next week, and I'd like to finish this seemingly endless painting. My daughter is being mysterious, and I don't know why."

"Alex, think about it for a minute. Why would a married daughter want to meet with her father regarding something you say is mysterious, especially if she didn't sound upset?"

He said, "Actually, she seemed happy." Pausing for a minute, he said, "You think so?"

"For a guy with two daughters and other women in his life, you can be naïve. Let's plan your trip for three weeks from now."

Alex said, "She's also coming here to grill me about you having stayed here. My other daughter spoke to her."

"I sense they are close, which means they can double team you. Tell Merry I'm glad for her and am sorry we didn't meet. Call me and let me know if I'm right."

On Saturday, Merry arrived mid-morning; Alex watched his daughter's face. He knew Carolyn was right: Merry's smile stretched across her face, the first hint of the news. She charged toward her father and hugged him so hard, he released a puff of air.

"Sit down," she instructed him, and sat in a chair across from him. "I'm pregnant!" Merry exclaimed.

They both stood and embraced again. "I'm so happy for you," Alex said.

Merry explained the specifics: the results of the home pregnancy test, the physician's confirmation, and the projected due date. "Now you know why I couldn't help you paint. The smell would make me sick."

"Have you chosen a name yet?"

Merry laughed. "You met Bradley's parents; they're wonderful people but superstitious. They believe naming a child too early is bad luck. Regardless, Bradley and I do feel it's too soon, although I've had one suggestion already."

"Let me guess; if it's a girl: Bethany."

"You know your other daughter. Now that I've given you all the information about my pregnancy, it's your turn to explain."

Alex described the reason for Carolyn's visit, the problem she encountered getting a hotel, and his room offer. "Bethany came over to pick up some clothes, and she met Carolyn."

"The way she explained, I would have thought she caught you two *en flagrante*."

"We were in pajamas and bathrobe and having breakfast. Carolyn talked to Bethany for a while. It was all innocent. We both know your sister exaggerates."

"I wouldn't put it past her, but I also think she was hoping you had someone who could be in your life."

"Carolyn will be in my life, but platonically. I enjoy being with her and don't want to lose that. In a few weeks, I'll be driving to her area, and we can spend time together."

"That's great, but you need a woman who is more than a buddy."

"I've been thinking a lot lately and realize I can't live like this: no job, no love life."

"Dad, you decided to retire and not date, and you can undecide both. Mom's gone; I've gotten past the grief, never forgetting her, but also never allowing her memory to dilute all the positive things in my life, like you. I blamed you for the divorce, and by extension, for her death. I know I was wrong and regret the time I pulled away from you. But now we all can look forward to the child. I have my husband and Bethany has Bradley. You have no one to love outside of family." The tears overflowed her lower lashes. Alex's eyes moistened.

His daughter stayed until late afternoon and promised she would give him periodic updates on her pregnancy.

~ * ~

Alex packed for his trip to see Carolyn. They'd spoken a few times and were eager for the day. She'd cleared her schedule for Monday, leaving three days to spend without interruption. The sun had cut through thin clouds, and the weather was warm. As he drove, Alex saw planted fields and large tracts of greening soil. Tree buds had exploded to life, and people were bicycling along the streets. When he arrived at her house, Carolyn came out to greet him.

For the first few hours, they provided updates on their lives for the short time since they last met. Alex shared Merry was starting to show, and since Bradley was near full recovery, he and Bethany were traveling to the region where they would be living while in graduate school. Carolyn spoke about her son.

"Did you finish painting?"

"Yes, the house looks wonderful. The last time you were there, the wedding took a lot of our time. Next time you come—and I hope there is a next time—I would like your thoughts on getting the house ready for a sale. I know I mentioned the idea when you were last at my place, but it was just a thought; now I'm ready to consider selling. I've been surprised my daughters are so strong about the matter."

"Alex, I don't want to play amateur psychologist, but you used the word 'house' repeatedly and not 'home.' Perhaps you are ready to leave."

He said nothing for a while, staring past her. "You're very perceptive."

"Okay, how good are you at grilling? I filled the tank, cleaned off the grill, and bought steaks," she said to redirect the serious conversation.

"Is that a question or a subtle challenge?"

"Take it however you want, but I'm hungry."

Stepping onto the deck, he looked at the row of trees at the far end of her yard and started the grill. Carolyn came out, handing him the raw meat and a glass of red wine.

Putting her hand on his shoulder, she said, "It's warm enough to eat out here," pointing to the covered table at the other end of the deck.

Over the next few days, they drove through the area, went to a movie in town, hiked through a trail north of town, and spent long segments of the daytime doing little. They went to a local restaurant and ordered takeout the final night. Each night, they retired, they kissed lightly. On the second night, she removed her makeup before joining Alex on the couch to watch television. When Carolyn got up to make popcorn, Alex watched her until she was out of sight.

He tossed and turned at night and heard her get up early the last day.

In front of his car, he put his arms around Carolyn, said, "Being with you is so easy and relaxing."

She nodded and opened her mouth to say something.

"What is it?"

"Nothing; you'd better get going—don't forget it's a weekday, and you might hit traffic."

"I'll call you, and we can discuss your trip to my house. I'll invite Merry, so you'll have met both my daughters."

"Sure," Carolyn said and turned to walk back into the house.

A week later, Alex called her on her home phone and her cell. She didn't return either. Stumped, he tried again but got a message on his cell, apologizing that work was busy. Alex knew she had an unstructured work schedule, meeting with sellers at their convenience at night or on weekends, always on the buyers' schedule, but he was convinced she would have an opportunity to call him back. After a third attempt, he was annoyed and determined he wouldn't call or text her again. She was ignoring him, but he didn't know why.

He constantly communicated with his daughters and didn't mention the disappointment in not hearing from Carolyn. When he saw Merry's car pull into the driveway, Bethany got out of the passenger side. He smiled when Merry closed the driver's side door; she was wearing a loose blouse that stretched out a bit.

The sisters greeted him with a combined hug. Stepping back, Alex asked, "Okay, what's up. I love seeing you. Especially at the same time, but—"

"No special reason. How are things with Carolyn? I'd love to meet her," Merry said.

"She's fine, but you two aren't being honest."

The sisters looked at each other, and Bethany answered.

"Merry and I sensed something was wrong after you returned from seeing Carolyn. We assumed something happened. Have you been in touch?"

"You two know me. The three days I was with her were great, and I mentioned Carolyn should come here next time. I haven't heard from her since."

"Did you say anything that might have upset her? Remember, you were with two other women; did you tell her much about that?" Merry asked.

"No, I mentioned it briefly after the wedding, but not since. I told her I enjoyed seeing her and that it was easy being with her."

"Let's recap," Merry said. "You wanted to schedule a time to see each other again, and you said you were comfortable because she was easy to be with."

Bethany jumped in, "Did you say things like that often?"

"Yes, I wanted Carolyn to understand how much I enjoyed seeing her. Where are you going with this?"

"Do you want to answer, Bethany, or should I?" Merry asked.

"He's not getting it yet, but you're on a roll, so continue," Bethany answered.

Alex's head swiveled between his daughters.

"You schedule a time to get a haircut or go to the dentist. When you want to see Bethany or me, do you text first and fix the date? Did we contact you before we showed up today? What separates a platonic relationship from a romantic one is spontaneity.

"We may ask if you'll be home before we come, but do we break out calendars, and if there is a conflict, which appointment do we cancel? The answer's obvious. I know you didn't mean it the way she may have interpreted that she's *easy* to be with, but you're conveying you don't have deep feelings toward her, and that may not be the way she feels."

"Didn't you two discourage me from the whole pursuit of going backward, as you called it? More recently, didn't you push me to move on, look to the future rather than the past?" He didn't realize his voice was rising.

"Dad, don't be upset; we're concerned because we love you."

Merry said, "You need to assess your feelings about Carolyn, or maybe all the women in your past should stay there. I'm glad you went through the *adventure* and experienced emotions and desires long dormant in some ways. Now you can seek someone new with expectation and no history, knowing more about being involved."

"I need to think hard about both: my feelings toward Carolyn and what I should do going from now on. I'm glad you both care about me and can be candid, and now I need to be honest with myself."

~ * ~

Over the next few days, Alex thought about little else but what was the next move, starting out with seeing other women. The suggestion his daughters made—and Maria had repeated—was to put the past and most recent connections behind him. He realized they were right, but having recognized that, wondered *what do I do about it*. When he shared his latest conclusion with Bethany, she offered advice.

"Dad, there are dating websites, including some with people your age."

Hours later, his younger daughter called again and gave him a list of what she named "Senior web addresses."

Alex, certain that Bethany had contacted her sister, knew he would be hearing from Merry. It didn't take long. In some ways, her guidance contradicted Bethany's. "A lot of people post twenty-year-old photographs or exaggerate their background or lie." However, she mentioned a source that struck a chord. "You must know single women among friends, former co-workers, clients and even neighbors."

The next day, he looked through his old work files for a listing of women who worked for him. Scrolling down the list, his finger stopped at Anne Acquilina. She was one of his most successful agents, with the most contagious smile that charmed clients regardless of their age or gender. In the agency's early days, Allex would invite all the reps to his house for a cookout, and his wife prepared all the ingredients and tended to guests. He remembered Pietrina called Anne "sweet-faced."

He hoped her phone number hadn't changed from the listing and called Anne and she picked up on the first ring.

"Hi, Alex; it's so good to hear from you," she said in her familiar upbeat tone.

After returning the greeting, he went directly to the reason for the call. "I'd like to see you; it's been a while." He stumbled over the purpose, but she spared him.

"I'd love to meet with you and we can talk over old times." With her voice lowered as if concerned with being overheard, she added, "I can share what's been happening at the agency since you left."

They arranged to dine at a restaurant near to the agency location. When he passed his former office, he felt a bit of sadness. Anne was waiting outside the restaurant when he approached. She hugged him and, stepping back, said, "I'd say you haven't changed since you left, but it wasn't that long ago, although we haven't seen each other in at least a year."

"You look lovely, Anne."

She waved her hand as if batting away the compliment.

When they were seated inside, Alex looked around and said, "I've closed a lot of deals here."

"Me too," Anne chirped. She reached across the table and put her hands on Alex's wrists. "I'm sorry about Pietrina. She was a delightful woman and so gracious."

"Thank you, and I am grateful you were at her wake."

"Along with everyone from the office and field, especially us old-timers who had met her."

While they ate, Anne asked: "What have you been doing since you sold the business?"

Alex explained he traveled to see old friends without elaborating; in the following pause, Anne talked about her newer clients, including a man who rubbed her knee when she was going over the forms with him. She mentioned other reps they both knew. Pausing, Anne said, "Are you listening? You keep looking away."

Alex looked at her. "I'm sorry. Being so near to the office and eating at a place where I'd been often. I'm trying to get away from the past."

Anne snickered. "I'm part of your past."

Alex stuttered, and his face reddened. "No, no. I don't think of you that way. I was looking forward to seeing you."

"Alex, I know how hard it is to get back into dating, especially after someone you loved is gone. My husband didn't die, but he was out of my life after the divorce."

"I didn't explain about the trips to meet old friends and that they—the three—were women I had serious relationships with before I met Pietrina. I guess I was looking for familiarity."

"But the recent times didn't lead to a renewed relationship, so familiarity didn't work as a criterion."

"We've not even had dessert and you figured me out."

They finished dinner and had coffee as the last portion of the meal.

Outside the restaurant, they stopped. "I figured since we were dining nearby, I went to the office first to complete some paperwork. My car is over there," Anne said, pointing.

"I screwed up this time, but I'd like to see you again—"

"I don't think that's best. There's no spark, or whatever term describes what's missing. I wondered if something could develop between us, but I was wrong. When you are in the right frame of mind, you'll be a great person to be with." She extended her hand.

Alex grabbed the outstretched hand and squeezed gently. "It was good to see you, Anne."

~ * ~

Stunned by Anne's insight, Alex thought about little else, asking himself questions and sorting through answers. He recognized that the relationships with Maddy and Maria were over. As much as he was grateful for the days with each, there was no future.

But what about Carolyn? Did he want a romantic involvement or a friendship? Was she also someone he was drawn to because of familiarity? He recalled the moments when he looked at her and felt pleasure in her proximity, and when they stayed at the motel in the same room, he knew he had experienced more than companionship. Carolyn once said they touched a lot, and when they danced at the reception, he'd felt her body against his. Alex chastised himself as egotistic, assuming he could rekindle old emotions and connections with three women, the self-centered parallel to the tv show others mentioned: *The Batchelor*.

He realized he'd dealt with a lot of endings: his marriage, his ex-wife's death, his business, and the contact with Maddy and Maria was added to the list. His positive memory of the two women, which was the rationale for beginning his so-called 'adventure', was now altered by the recent experiences. But would the same be said about Carolyn? Could he withstand another failure if he attempted to pursue that relationship further, and was that the wisest decision on behalf of them both? Had Carolyn closed that door already?

When he pondered those questions, a simple feeling was strengthening—he missed Carolyn.

A week later, Alex called Mark Rider, the man who bought his business and scheduled a meeting time. Arriving at his former office and walking up to the desk where his secretary once sat, he told the young woman he had an appointment. Mark came out with his hand extended to shake and lead him inside.

"Your former staff has been asking about you; some of your clients as well. What have you been doing since you retired?"

"Been traveling mostly, but I've been bored lately."

Mark laughed. "Are you looking for a job?"

"Not exactly," Alex answered. He explained at length while Mark listened, not showing a reaction, but when Alex finished, Mark smiled and said, "That's fine with me."

They continued discussing for another half hour, and Alex left, pleased with the outcome.

On Wednesday, he called his daughters and asked them to come down that weekend, which led to several questions from both; he refused to answer before they arrived. He imagined the conversations between the two, speculating on his motive for assembling.

Bethany traveled the shorter distance and tried unsuccessfully to pump Alex before her sister arrived, as she'd done in the past. They chatted when Merry entered the house, but she wanted to "Get right to it."

Alex knew he had caught them by surprise because they had never interrupted or questioned him until he finished. However, when he was done, the two young women talked over each other to ask for more specifics. During one part of his answers, Bethany's eyes filled up, and Merry went into the kitchen for water. "I wanted to wait before doing anything else until next weekend, so you have time to absorb everything."

"You are right, Dad. I need to go home, think about everything you said, and talk to my husband," Merry said.

"I agree with Merry. We are surprised, and I don't know what to say right now, so I'm going, too. We love you."

"I understand; explain to your significant others. I'm always here if you want to talk further."

Twelve

Alex rose early on Sunday after a restless night. In summer, the sun warmed the light wind and dried the ground after a gentle overnight rain. He stopped for gas and continued to his destination. When he arrived, he pulled into her driveway. Carolyn opened the door after he knocked, the surprise showing on her face.

"What are you doing here?"

"Since you didn't return my calls, I decided to try in person," Alex answered. "The old saying about Mohammed and the mountain."

"First, come in; you have to explain more than returning a phone call."

Carolyn sat on the couch. Her face was free of makeup, and she wore jeans and a short-sleeved blouse. When he sat beside her, Carolyn squirmed. "Not too close. I look horrible. Sunday is my cleaning day, and I haven't showered—"

"You're still beautiful," he said as he touched her face. "I know this is crazy, but I had to see you and want to continue seeing you."

"I'm sorry I haven't returned your calls; it was a tough decision, but I don't want to be the sole survivor of your adventure. You told me those other relationships, once a part of your life, would not be part of your future, and I felt I was the consolation prize for all the trips, brief re-involvements, and their failures. You thought I could offer a friendship, but I don't want that. Remember me as a high school girl you once knew and let that be enough while you seek...”

Alex cut her off again. “No, no,” he gestured furiously, “ I cared for Maddy and Maria, but those feelings blended with a remembered love and the recent reconnection to the point I couldn't separate one from the other.”

Why wouldn't it be the same with me?"

“Since we were last together, I've thought about being with you constantly. When we were first involved, we were kids talking about love when we didn't know what the words meant. I love you now and fully understand what those words mean.

“I met with Maddy and Maria at a time in my life and theirs when we couldn't commit, and the possibility had passed. Of course, their lives are much more complex, and the obstacles were significant, less so for me. I don't doubt that those recent memories will fade for them and me.

“I like to believe Maddy, Maria and I benefitted from those brief times together because they helped us better understand what we wanted and needed. But I should have stopped the other trips after seeing you and taken more time to be with you.

“I went over the times I was with you and realized my feelings for you had increased. I was tongue-tied around you at the reunion. At the motel in Charlottesville, I looked at you, and my thoughts of you in the other bed weren't platonic. You even said we were physical with each other, holding hands, kissing. Yes, I’m comfortable with you, but that’s a good thing; because I enjoy being with you doesn’t mean my feelings for you don’t run deep. I really want a relationship with you, but if it wasn't what you wanted, I would look for the ease and attraction that I have with you."

Carolyn interrupted him. "I wished you had said so or acted on your emotions before."

Alex smiled and continued. "I also thought about the incident with the older couple and the damage to their house. I don't doubt that you do your best for clients, but how you cared for them burdened yourself with unrequired guilt, and tended to their upset was unique and impressive. When we met them after they returned, I saw your eyes fill as you comforted and reassured them. The way you care about people and feel responsible for others is exceptional. I thought how fortunate I would be as a recipient of that caring, as would my family. However, if you feel our relationship needs to be assigned to the past, I'll leave and won't contact you again. But it's not what I want."

"Alex, I remembered you when we first reconnected, and some of those feelings from long ago came back, but they say you never forget your first love, and maybe that was true with you. If you love me, it must be solely for what I am now and not in the past."

He smiled. "The memories were so wonderful, but my love for you is based on what I feel today and the desire to be with you now. We were so much to each other in high school, but those recollections are only a small part of my feelings now; I need you in my life and future."

Carolyn threw her arms around him and kissed him. "I love you, too. I've been unhappy all this time, thinking I'd never see you again, but staying solely as friends would have been painful."

They embraced; she rested her head on his shoulder and said, "You mentioned that those other women—Maddy and Maria—had personal obstacles, but I don't have any. I'm not married, and my career won't be in the way of a relationship between us. Does that make me more appealing?"

Alex said, "Continuing our relationship has barriers. You live far from me, and I have to make life changes to be with you, and I will."

Carolyn said, "I mentioned the whole quest was like an episode of *The Batchelor*. Doesn't the man get to sleep with the three finalists?" She led him to her bedroom. On the way, she said, "I will not ask you if you slept with the other two—not yet, anyway."

Later in bed, she said, "How do we make this work? Do we keep traveling back and forth between houses on weekends? I'd like us to be with each other more than that." Carolyn turned toward him to hear his response.

"I'm going to sell my house. You have a job here, and I don't want to disrupt your life; I'm much freer to move. There's more. I'm getting restless and need something to keep me busy while you work. I spoke to the man who purchased my agency, and he doesn't have any concerns if I start a business in town here since I'd be too distant to violate the non-compete agreement I signed as part of the sale. He would even recommend a small manufacturer in the region he knew was seeking a new broker. I'll have to go back and forth for a while, especially to sell the house, but I'm hoping you'll go with me often."

"You have thought this through. What if we'd decided not to try?"

"I haven't sold the house nor applied for a local broker's license, so there is nothing I would need to reverse. Besides, I have to move some day; the house is too big for one person."

Carolyn laughed. "Pretty self-assured, aren't you? Alex, I'm reluctant to ask. How do your children feel about the future changes? You'll be moving away from them and selling the house they grew up in."

"They're fine with it. The distance isn't so great from here. Merry is having a baby and she and her husband will be very busy. Bethany is going away to graduate school with a man who will be her husband in a few weeks. After she got over the shock of finding us in my house, both wearing pajamas, my younger daughter realized we were good for each other. Merry needs to make her own decisions, and she'll likely grill you like a seasoned detective. I want you to meet my entire family. My daughters want this to work and have helped me realize things."

"Do you think you'll have it easy with my son? Think again."

They both laughed and settled back on the pillows in an embrace.

"Did you bring a suitcase?" Carolyn asked.

Alex nodded. "I was a boy scout and learned to be prepared."

"You've earned a merit badge from me," she said coyly. "Why don't you get your luggage while I shower." On the way to the bathroom, Carolyn stopped, grinned, and said, "Do you have any more ex-girlfriends out there?"

Meet James Hanley

Jim Hanley was born in Brooklyn, New York, moved to Long Island, NY after a stint in the military, and recently relocated to Maryland. Jim Hanley's background includes careers in the military, human resources, and as an adjunct professor. He has had over ninety short stories published in print and online magazines.

Jim started writing short stories in various genres and later transitioned to novels in the Western and mystery styles. *Seeking the Future in the Past* is his first romance work, and he is currently drafting another.

Dear reader,

I hope you've enjoyed reading this tale of visits to the
past.

Your opinion is valuable to other
readers like you,
who may be looking for books like mine.

Please consider taking a few minutes to post a review,
however brief,
on the site where you purchased this book
or on the Wings ePress web page.

You may also want to visit my author page
at the Wings' website, where you can find
all the other books in my series.

Thank you!

Jim Hanley

Visit Our Website
*For The Full Inventory
Of Quality Books:*

<u>Wings ePress, Inc</u>

*Quality trade paperbacks and downloads
in multiple formats,
in genres ranging from light romantic comedy to
general fiction and horror.
Wings has something for every reader's taste.
Visit the website, then bookmark it.*
We add new titles each month!

*Wings ePress, Inc.
3000 N. Rock Road
Newton, KS 67114*